P9-DHP-768

"Mariella? What is it? What's wrong?" she heard Xavier demanding angrily. "If you feel unwell..."

"No, I'm fine," she began, and then stopped, unable to drag her gaze away from his mouth, where it had focused with hungry, yearning intensity.

She could feel the hot burn of his gaze as it dropped to her own mouth. She was trembling, her whole body galvanized by tiny sensual ripples of reaction and awareness that made her sway slightly towards him. She felt him shudder as he drew breath into his lungs, her body instinctively leaning into his as weakness washed over her.

His mouth touched her, but not in the way she had remembered it doing before.

Caught up in the shock of what she had experienced, Mariella lifted her hand to touch her own lips, as though unable to believe what had happened...what she had wanted to happen. She had wanted Xavier to kiss her; her body ached for him in a hundred intimate ways that held her in silent shock. She and Xavier were enemies, weren't they?

Arabian Nights

by
Penny Jordan

Spent at the sheikh's pleasure...

The Sheikh's Virgin Bride #2325
One Night with the Sheikh #2332

Welcome back to the exotic land of Zuran,
a beautiful romantic place
where anything is possible.

Experience a night of passion
under a desert moon
in Harlequin Presents®.

Penny Jordan

ONE NIGHT WITH THE SHEIKH

Arabian Nights

HARLEQUIN®

TORONTO • NEW YORK • LONDON
AMSTERDAM • PARIS • SYDNEY • HAMBURG
STOCKHOLM • ATHENS • TOKYO • MILAN • MADRID
PRAGUE • WARSAW • BUDAPEST • AUCKLAND

If you purchased this book without a cover you should be aware that this book is stolen property. It was reported as "unsold and destroyed" to the publisher, and neither the author nor the publisher has received any payment for this "stripped book."

ISBN 0-373-12332-9

ONE NIGHT WITH THE SHEIKH

First North American Publication 2003.

Copyright © 2003 by Penny Jordan.

All rights reserved. Except for use in any review, the reproduction or utilization of this work in whole or in part in any form by any electronic, mechanical or other means, now known or hereafter invented, including xerography, photocopying and recording, or in any information storage or retrieval system, is forbidden without the written permission of the publisher, Harlequin Enterprises Limited, 225 Duncan Mill Road, Don Mills, Ontario, Canada M3B 3K9.

All characters in this book have no existence outside the imagination of the author and have no relation whatsoever to anyone bearing the same name or names. They are not even distantly inspired by any individual known or unknown to the author, and all incidents are pure invention.

This edition published by arrangement with Harlequin Books S.A.

® and TM are trademarks of the publisher. Trademarks indicated with ® are registered in the United States Patent and Trademark Office, the Canadian Trade Marks Office and in other countries.

Visit us at www.eHarlequin.com

Printed in U.S.A.

PROLOGUE

'YOU won't forget your mummy whilst I'm away working, will you, my precious baby girl?'

Mariella watched sympathetically as her younger half-sister Tanya's eyes filled with tears as she handed her precious four-month-old daughter over to her.

'I know that Fleur couldn't have anyone better to look after her than you, Ella,' Tanya acknowledged emotionally. 'After all, you became my mother as well as my sister when Mum and Dad died. I just wish I could have got a job that didn't mean I have to be away, but this six-week contract on this cruise liner pays so well that I just can't afford to give it up! Yes, I know you would support us both,' she continued before Mariella could say anything, 'but that isn't what I want. I want to be as independent as I can be. Anyway,' she told Mariella bitterly, 'supporting Fleur financially should be her father's job and not yours! What I ever saw in that weak, lying rat of a man, I'll never know! My wonderful sexy dream fantasy of a sheikh! Some dream he turned out to be—more of a nightmare.'

Mariella let her vent her feelings, without comment, knowing just how devastated and hurt her half-sister had been when her lover had abandoned her.

'You don't have to do this, Tanya,' she told her gently now. 'I'm earning enough to support us all, and this house is big enough for the three of us.'

'Oh, Mariella, I know that. I know you'd starve

yourself to give to me and Fleur, but that isn't what I
want. You've done so much for me since Mum and
Dad died. You were only eighteen, after all, three years
younger than I am now, when we found out that there
wasn't going to be any money! I suppose Dad wanted
to give us all so much that he simply didn't think about
what would happen if anything happened to him, and
with him remortgaging the house because of the stock
market crisis.'

Silently the sisters looked at one another.

Both of them had inherited their mother's delicate
bone structure and heart-shaped face, along with her
strawberry-blonde hair and peach perfect complexion,
but where Tanya had inherited her father's height and
hazel eyes, Mariella had inherited intensely turquoise
eyes from her father, the man who had decided less
than a year after her birth that the responsibilities of
fatherhood and marriage simply weren't for him and
walked out on his wife and baby daughter.

'It's not fair,' Tanya had mock complained to her
when she had announced that she was not going to go
to university as Mariella had hoped she would, but
wanted to pursue a career singing and dancing. 'If I
had your eyes, I'd have a ready-made advantage over
everyone else whenever I went for a part.'

Although she knew how headstrong and impulsive
her half-sister could be, Mariella admired her for what
she was doing, even whilst she worried about how she
was going to cope with being away from her daughter
for six long weeks.

Whatever small differences there might ever have
been between them, in their passionate and protective
love for baby Fleur they were totally united.

'I'll ring every day,' Tanya promised chokily.

'And I want to know everything she does, Ella...
Every tiny little thing. Oh, Ella...I feel so guilty about
all of this...I know how you suffered as a little girl
because your father wasn't there; because he'd abandoned you and Mum...and I know too how lucky I
was to have both Mum and Dad and you there for me,
and yet here is my poor little Fleur...'

Holding Fleur in one arm, Mariella hugged her sister
tightly with the other.

'The taxi's here,' she warned, before releasing Tanya
and tenderly brushing the tears off her face.

'Ella! I've got the most fab commission for you.'

Recognising the voice of her agent, Mariella shifted
Fleur's warm weight from one arm to the other, smiling
lovingly at her as the baby guzzled happily on her bottle. 'It's racehorses, dozens of them. The client owns
his own racing yard out in Zuran. He's a member of
the Zuran royal family, and apparently he heard about
you via that chap in Kentucky, whose Kentucky Derby
winner you painted the other year. Anyway—he wants
to fly you out there, all expenses paid, so that you can
discuss the project with him, see the beasts *in situ* so
to speak!'

Mariella laughed. Kate, with her immaculate designer clothes and equally immaculate all-white apartment, was not an animal lover. 'Ella, what is that
noise?' she demanded plaintively.

Mariella laughed. 'It's Fleur. I'm just giving her her
bottle. It does sound promising, but right now I'm
pretty booked with commissions, and, to be honest, I
don't really think that going to Zuran is on. For a start,
I'm looking after Fleur for the next six weeks, and—'

'That's no problem—I am sure Prince Sayid

wouldn't mind you taking her with you and February is the perfect time of year to go there; the weather will be wonderful—warm and mild. Ella, you can't turn this one down. Just what I'd earn in commission is making my mouth water,' she admitted frankly.

Ella laughed. 'Ah, I see...'

She had begun painting animal 'portraits' almost by accident. Her painting had been merely a small hobby and her 'pet portraits' done for friends, but her reputation had spread by word of mouth, and eventually she had decided to make it her full-time career.

Now she earned what to her was a very comfortable living from her work, and she knew she would normally have leapt at the chance she was being offered.

'I'd love to go, Kate,' she replied. 'But Fleur is my priority right now...'

'Well, don't turn it down out of hand,' Kate warned her. 'Like I said, there's no reason why Fleur shouldn't go with you. You won't be working on this trip, it's only a mutual look-see. You'd be gone just over a week, and forget any idiotic ideas you might have about potential health hazards to any young baby out there—Zuran is second to none when it comes to being a world-class cosmopolitan city!'

One of the reasons Mariella had originally bought her small three-storey house had been because of the excellent north-facing window on the top floor, which she had turned into her studio. With Fleur contently fed she looked out at the grey early February day. The rain that had been sheeting down all week had turned to a mere drizzle. A walk in the park and some fresh air would do them both good, Mariella decided, putting Fleur down whilst she went to prepare her pram.

It had been her decision to buy the baby a huge old-fashioned 'nanny' style pram.

'You can use the running stroller if you want,' she had informed Tanya firmly. 'But when I walk her it will be in a traditional vehicle and at a traditional pace!'

'Ella, you talk as though you were sixty-eight, not twenty-eight,' Tanya had protested. Perhaps she was a little bit old-fashioned, Mariella conceded as she started to remove the blankets from the running stroller to put in the pram. Her father's desertion and her mother's consequent vulnerability and helplessness had left her with a very strong determination to stand on her own two feet, and an extremely strong disinclination to allow herself to be emotionally vulnerable through loving a man too much as her mother had done.

After all, as Tanya had proved, it was possible to inherit a tendency!

She frowned as her fingers brushed against a balled-up piece of paper as she removed the bedding. It could easily have scratched Fleur's delicate skin. She was on the point of throwing it away, when a line of her sister's handwriting suddenly caught her eye.

The piece of paper was a letter, Mariella recognised, and she could see the name and address on it quite plainly.

'Sheikh Xavier Al Agir, No. 24, Quaffire Beach Road, Zuran City.'

Her heart thudded guiltily as she smoothed out the note and read the first line.

'You have destroyed my life and Fleur's and I shall hate you for ever for that,' she read.

The letter was obviously one Tanya had written but not sent to Fleur's father.

Fleur had always refused to discuss her relationship with him other than to say that he was a very wealthy Middle Eastern man whom she had met whilst working in a nightclub as a singer and dancer.

Privately Mariella had always thought that he had escaped far too lightly from his responsibility to her sister and to his baby...

And now she had discovered he lived in Zuran! Frowning slightly, she carefully folded the note. She had no right to interfere, she knew that, but... Would she be interfering or merely acknowledging the validity of fate? How many, many times over the years had she longed for the opportunity to confront her own father and tell him just what she thought of him, how he had broken her mother's heart and almost destroyed her life?

Her father, like her mother, was now dead, and could never make reparation for what he had done; but Tanya's lover was very much alive, and it would give her a great deal of satisfaction to tell him just what she thought of him!

Blowing Fleur a kiss, she hurried over to the telephone and quickly dialled her agent's number.

'Kate,' she began. 'I've been thinking...about that trip to Zuran...'

'You've changed your mind! Wonderful... You won't regret it Ella, I promise you. I mean, this guy is mega, mega rich, and what he's prepared to pay to have his four-legged friends immortalised in oils...'

Listening to her, Mariella reflected ruefully that on occasion Kate could show a depressing tendency to favour the material over the emotional, but she was an excellent agent!

CHAPTER ONE

ZURAN had to have the cleanest airport in the world, Mariella decided as she retrieved her luggage and headed for the exit area, and Kate had been right about Prince Sayid's willingness to spare no expense to get her to Zuran. In the first-class cabin of their aircraft Fleur had been treated like a little princess!

Arrangements had been made for her to be chauffeur-driven to the Beach Club Resort where she would be staying along with Fleur in their own private bungalow, and, thanks to the prince's influence with the right diplomatic departments, all the necessary arrangements to get Fleur a passport, with Tanya's permission, had also been accomplished at top speed!

Craning her neck, Mariella looked round the busy arrivals area searching for someone carrying a placard bearing her name.

Behind her she was vaguely aware of something going on, not so much because of an increase in the noise level but rather because of the way it suddenly fell away. Alerted by some sixth sense, Mariella turned round, her eyes widening as she watched the way the crowds parted to make way for the small phalanx of white-robed men. Like traditional outriders, they carved a wide path through the crowd to allow the man striding behind them to cross the marble floor unhindered. Taller than the others, he looked neither to the right nor the left so that Mariella's artist's eye was able

11

to observe the patrician arrogance of a profile that could only belong to a man used to being in command.

Instinctively, without being able to substantiate her reaction, Mariella didn't like him. He was too arrogant, too aware of his own importance. So physically and powerfully male, perfect in a way that sent a hundred unwanted sexual messages skittering over her suddenly very sensitive nerve endings. He had drawn level with her, and, whether because she sensed her antagonism or because Mariella had gripped her just a little bit more tightly, Fleur suddenly broke the silence with a small cry.

Instantly the dark head turned in their direction whilst the equally dark eyes burned into Mariella's. Mariella registered his gaze as her body gave a small, tight shudder.

The dark eyes stripped her, not of her clothes, but of her skin, her defences, Mariella recognised shakily, leaving them shredded down to her bones; her soul! But his gaze lingered longest of all on her face. Her eyes, she realised as she returned his remote and disdainful look of contempt with one of smouldering fury.

Fleur made another small sound and immediately his gaze switched from her to the baby and stayed there for a while, before it switched back to her own as though checking something.

Whatever it had been it brought a sneering look of contempt to his mouth that curved it into an even more dangerous line, Mariella noticed as her body responded to his reaction with a slow burn of colour along her cheekbones.

How dared he look at her with such contempt? She didn't care who or what he was! Once she imagined her father must have looked so at her mother before

walking out on her, before leaving her to sink into the
needy despair and dependence that Mariella remembered so starkly from her childhood, until her stepfather
with his love and kindness had come to lift them both
out of the dark, mean place her father had left them in.

As swiftly and as silently as they had arrived the
small group of men swept through the hall and left. As
a production it had been ridiculously overdone and theatrical, Mariella decided as she found the chauffeur patiently waiting for her and allowed herself to be carefully driven along with Fleur in the air-conditioned
luxury of the limousine.

The Beach Club Resort was everything a five-star resort should be and more, Mariella acknowledged a couple of hours later when she had finished her exploration
of her new surroundings.

The bungalow she had been allocated had two large
bedrooms, each with its own bathroom, a small kitchen
area, a living room, a private patio complete with
whirlpool, but it was the obvious forethought that had
gone into equipping the place for a very young baby
that most impressed Mariella. A good-sized cot had
been provided and placed next to the bed, the bathroom
was equipped with what was obviously a brand-new
baby bath, baby toiletries had been added to the luxurious range provided for her own use, and in the fridge
was a very full selection of top-of-the-range baby
foods. However, it was the letter that had been left for
her stating that the Beach Club's chef would prepare
fresh organic baby food for Fleur on request that really
made Mariella feel she could relax.

Having settled Fleur, who fell asleep as easily and
comfortably as though she was in her own home,

Mariella checked her watch and then put a call through to her sister. Tanya's cruise liner was on an extended tour of the Caribbean and the Gulf of Mexico.

'Ella, how's Fleur?' Tanya demanded immediately.

'Fast asleep,' Mariella told her. 'She was fine on the flight and got thoroughly spoiled. How are you?'

'Oh…fine… Very busy…we're doing two shows each evening, with no time off, but as I said the money is excellent. Ella, I must go… Give Fleur a big kiss for me.'

A little guiltily, Mariella looked at the now-silent mobile. She hadn't said anything to Tanya about her determination to confront her sister's faithless ex-lover and tell him just what she thought about him! Tanya might have gone willingly to his bed, but Mariella knew she hadn't been lying to her when she had told her that she had believed that he loved her, and that they had a future together.

Mariella struggled to wake up from a confused and disjointed dream in which she was being dragged by her guards to lie trembling at the feet of the man who was now her master. How she hated him. Hated him for the way he stood there towering over her, looking down at her, looking over her so thoroughly that she felt as though his gaze burned her flesh.

He was looking deep into her eyes. His were the colour of the storm-tossed skies and seas of her homeland, a cold, pure grey that chilled her through and through.

'You dare to challenge me?' he was demanding softly as he moved closer to her. Behind her Mariella was conscious of the threatening presence of the guards.

She hated him with every sinew of her body, every pulse of blood from her heart. He left the divan where he had been sitting and came towards her, bending down, extending his hand to her face, but as his fingers gripped her chin Mariella turned her head and bit sharply into the soft pad of flesh below his thumb.

She felt the movement of the air as the guards leapt into action, heard them draw their swords, and her body waited for the welcome kiss of death, but instead the guards were dismissed whilst her tormentor stepped back from her. One bright spot of blood glistened on the intricately inlaid tiled floor.

'You are like a wildcat and as such need to be tamed,' she heard him telling her softly.

She could feel the cleanliness of her hair on her bare skin and froze as he slowly circled her, standing behind her and sliding his hand through her hair and then wrapping it tightly around his fingers, arching her back against his body so that her semi-naked breasts were thrown into taut profile. His free hand reached for the clasp securing her top and her whole body shook with outrage. And then abruptly he released her, turning to face her so that she could see the contempt in his eyes.

Swimming up through the layers of her dream Mariella recognised that his face was one she knew; that his cynical contempt was something she had experienced before...

In the half heartbeat of time between sleeping and waking she realised why. The man in her dream had been the arrogant, hawk-eyed man she had seen earlier at the airport!

Getting out of bed, she went into the bathroom, shaking her head to clear her thoughts, and then, when that tactic did nothing to subdue their dangerous, clinging tentacles of remembered sensuality, she turned on the shower, deliberately setting it at a punishing 'cool,' before stepping into it.

The minute the cool spray hit her overheated skin she shuddered, gritting her teeth as she washed the slick film from her body, and then stepping out of the shower, to wrap herself in a luxuriously thick, soft white towel. In the mirror in front of her she could see the pale, pearlescent gleam of her own skin, and dangerously she knew that if she were merely to close her eyes, behind her closed eyelids she would immediately see her tormentor, tall, cynically watchful, as he mocked her before reaching out to take the towel from her body and claim her.

Infuriated with herself, Mariella rubbed her damp skin roughly with the towel, and then re-set the air-conditioning. In her cot Fleur slept peacefully. Going to the fridge, Mariella removed a bottle of water and opened it. Her hand was shaking so much some of it slopped from the bottle onto the worktop.

Mariella and Fleur had just finished eating a leisurely breakfast on their private patio when a message came chattering through the fax machine. Frowning, Mariella read it. The prince had been called away on some unexpected business and would not now be able to see her for several days. He apologised to Mariella for having to change their arrangements, but asked her to enjoy the facilities of the Beach Club at his expense until his return.

Carefully smoothing sun-protection lotion onto Fleur's happy, wriggling little body, Mariella bent her head to kiss her tummy, acknowledging that this would be an ideal time to seek out Fleur's father. She had his address, after all! So all she needed to do was summon a taxi to take her there!

Kate had been quite correct when she had described Zuran's February weather as perfect, Mariella admitted half an hour later as she carried Fleur out into the warm sunshine. Since she was here on business and not holiday she had packed accordingly, and was wearing a pair of soft white linen trousers and a protective long-sleeved top. When she showed the taxi driver the sheikh's address he smiled and nodded. 'It will take maybe three quarters of an hour,' he told her. 'You have business with the sheikh?' he asked her conversationally.

Having learned already just how friendly people were, Mariella didn't take offence, replying simply tongue in cheek, 'You could say that.'

'He is a famous man. Revered by his tribe. They admire him for the way he has supported their right to live their lives in the traditional way. Although he is an extremely successful businessman it is said that he still prefers to live simply in the desert the way his people always have. He is a very good man.'

Mariella reflected inwardly that the picture the driver had just drawn for her was considerably at odds with the one she had gained from her half-sister.

Tanya had met the man in a nightclub, after all. Mariella had never liked the fact that Tanya worked there—although she had been employed as a singer, it openly advertised the sexual charms of its dancers, and Tanya had freely admitted that the majority of the customers were male.

And, certainly, during the twelve months they had been together, Mariella had never heard Tanya mention any predilection on her sexy sheikh's part to spend quality time in the middle of the desert! In fact, if she was honest, she had gained the impression that he was something of a 'playboy,' to use a perhaps now out-dated word.

It took just under forty minutes for them to reach the impressive white mansion, which the taxi driver assured her was the correct address.

A huge pair of locked wrought-iron gates prevented them from going any farther, but as if by magic an official stepped out of one of the pair of gatehouses that flanked the gates, and approached the car.

As firmly as she could Mariella explained that she wished to see the sheikh.

'I am sorry but he is not available,' the official informed her. 'He is away at the oasis at the moment and not expected back for some time.'

This was a complication Mariella had not been expecting. Fleur had woken up and was starting to grizzle a little.

'If you would care to leave a message?' the official was offering courteously.

Ruefully Mariella acknowledged inwardly that the nature of the message she wanted to give to the sheikh was better delivered in person!

Thanking him, she asked the taxi driver to take her back to the hotel.

'If you want, I can find someone to drive you to this oasis?' he suggested.

'You know where it is?' she questioned him.

He gave a small shrug. 'Sure! But you will need a four-wheel drive vehicle, as the track can be covered with sand.'

'Could I drive there myself?' Mariella asked him.

'It is possible, yes. It would take you two, maybe three hours. You wish me to give you the directions?'

It made more sense to drive to the oasis under her own steam than to go to the expense of paying a driver for the day as well as hiring a vehicle, Mariella decided.

'Please,' she agreed.

Methodically, Mariella checked through everything she had put on one side to pack into the four-wheel drive for her trip into the desert. The Beach Club's information desk staff had assured her that it would be perfectly safe for her to drive into the desert, and had attended to all the necessary formalities for her, including ensuring that a proper baby seat was provided for Fleur.

The trip should take her around three hours—four if she stopped off at the popular oasis resort for lunch as recommended by the Beach Club. But just in case she decided not to, they had provided her with a packed lunch in the form of a picnic hamper.

If it hadn't been for the serious purpose of her trip, she could quite easily have felt she were embarking on an exciting adventure, Mariella thought. Like everything else connected with the Beach Club, the four-wheel drive was immaculately clean and was even provided with its own mobile telephone!

The road into the desert was clearly marked, and turned out to be a well-built, smooth road that was so easy to navigate that Mariella quickly felt confident.

The secluded oasis where apparently the sheikh was staying was located in the Agir mountain range.

The light breeze, which had been just stirring the air when she had left the Beach Club, had increased

enough to whip a fine dust of sand over her vehicle
and the road itself within an hour of her setting out on
her journey. The sand particles were so fine that somehow they actually managed to find their way into the
four-wheel drive, despite the fact that Mariella had the
doors and windows firmly closed. She had left the main
road, now branched out onto a well-marked track
across the desert itself.

It was a relief when she reached the Bedouin village
marked on her map. It was market day and she had to
drive patiently behind a camel train through the village,
but fortunately it turned off towards the oasis itself,
allowing her to accelerate.

In another half an hour she would stop for some
lunch—if she hadn't reached the second oasis, marked
on her map, she and Fleur would have their picnic instead.

The height of the sand dunes had left her feeling
surprised and awed; they were almost a mountain range
in themselves. Fleur was awake and Mariella turned
off the radio to play her one of her favourite nursery
rhyme tapes, singing along to it.

It was taking her longer than she'd estimated to
reach the tourist base at the oasis where she had
planned to have lunch—it was almost two o'clock now
and she had expected to be there at one. A film of sand
dust had turned the sky a brassy red-gold colour, and
as she crested a huge sand dune and looked down into
the emptiness on the other side of it Mariella began to
panic slightly. Surely she should be able to at least see
the tourist base oasis from here?

Ruefully she reached for the vehicle's mobile, realising that it might be sensible to ask for help, but to
her dismay when she tried to make a call to the number

programmed into the phone the only response was a
fierce crackling sound. Stopping the vehicle she
reached for her own mobile, but it was equally inef-
fective.

The sky was even more obscured by sand now, the
wind hitting the vehicle with such force that it was
physically rocking it. As though sensing her disquiet
Fleur began to cry. She was hungry and needed changing, Mariella recognised, automatically attending to the
baby's needs whilst she tried to decide what she should
do.

It was impossible that she could be lost, of course.
The vehicle was fitted with a compass and she had been
given very detailed and careful instructions, which she
had followed to the letter.

So why hadn't she reached the tourist oasis?

Fleur ate her own meal eagerly, but Mariella discovered that she herself had lost her appetite!

And then just as she was beginning to feel truly
afraid she saw it! A line of camels swaying out of the
dust towards her led by a robed camel driver.

Relieved, Mariella drove towards the camel train. Its
leader was gravely polite. She had missed the turning
to the oasis, he explained, something that was easily
done with such a wind blowing sand across the track.
To her alarm he further explained that, because of the
sudden deterioration in the weather, all tourists had
been urged to return to the city instead of remaining in
the desert, but since Mariella had come so far her best
course of action now was to press on to her ultimate
destination, which he carefully showed her how to do
using the vehicle's compass.

Thanking him, she did as he had instructed her,
grimly checking and re-checking the compass as she

drove up and down what felt like an interminable series of the sand dunes until eventually, in the distance through the sand blowing against her windscreen, she could just about see the looming mass of the mountain range.

It was already four o'clock and the light seemed to be fading, a fact that panicked Mariella into driving a little faster. She had never dreamed that her journey would prove so hazardous and she was very much regretting having set out on it, but now at last its end was in sight.

It took her almost another hour of zigzagging across the sand dunes to reach the rocky thrust of the beginnings of the mountain range. The oasis was situated in a deep ravine, its escarpment so high that Mariella shuddered a little as she drove into its shadows. This was the last kind of place she had expected to appeal to the man who had been her sister's faithless lover.

Would his villa here be as palatial as his home in Zuran? Mariella frowned and checked as the ravine opened out and she saw the oasis ahead of her. Remote and beautiful in its own way, it was very obviously a place of deep solitude, the oasis itself enclosed with a fringing of palms illuminated by the eerie glow of the final rays of the setting sun. Shielding her eyes, Mariella stopped the vehicle to look around. Where was the villa? All she could see was one solitary pavilion tent! A good-sized pavilion, to be sure, but most definitely not a villa! Had she somehow got lost—again?

Fleur had started to cry, a cross, tired, hungry noise that alerted Mariella to the fact that for Fleur's sake if nothing else she needed to stop.

Carefully she drove the vehicle forward over the

treacherously boulder-rutted track, which seemed more like a dry river bed than a roadway! Sand blowing in from the desert was covering the boulders and the thin sparse grass of the oasis.

There was a vehicle parked several yards from the pavilion and Mariella stopped next to it.

A man was emerging from the pavilion, alerted to her arrival by the sound of her vehicle.

As he strode towards her, his robe caught by the strong wind and flattened against his body revealing a torso muscle structure that caused her to suck in her own stomach in sharply dangerous womanly response to its maleness.

And then he turned his head and looked at her, and the earth halted on its axis before swinging perilously in a sickening movement as Mariella recognised him.

It was the man from the airport. The man from her dream!

CHAPTER TWO

HIS hand was on the door handle of the four-wheel drive. Wrenching it open, he demanded angrily, 'Who the devil are you?'

He was looking at her eyes again, with that same look of biting contempt glittering in his own as he raked her with a gritty gaze.

'I'm looking for Sheikh Xavier Al Agir,' Mariella responded, returning his look with one of her own—plus interest!

'What? What do you want with him?'

He was curt to the point of rudeness, but then, given what she had already seen—and dreamed—of him, she wouldn't have expected anything else.

'What I want with him is no business of yours!' she told him angrily.

In her seat Fleur's cries grew louder.

Peering into the vehicle, he demanded in disbelief, 'You've brought a baby out in this?'

The disgust and anger in his voice made her face sting even more than the pieces of sand blown against it by the wind.

'What the hell possessed you? Didn't you hear the weather warning earlier? This area was reported as being strictly out of bounds to tourists because of the threat of sandstorms.'

Hot-faced, Mariella remembered how she had switched off the radio to play Fleur's tapes.

'I'm sorry if I've arrived at an inconvenient time,'

she responded sarcastically to cover her own discomfort, 'but if you could just give me directions for the Oasis Istafan, then—'

'This is the Oasis Istafan,' came back the immediate and cold response.

It was? Then?

'I want to see Sheikh Xavier Al Agir,' Mariella told him again, gathering her composure together. 'I presume he is here?'

'What do you want to see him for?'

Mariella had had enough. 'That is no business of yours,' she said angrily. Inwardly she was worrying how on earth she was going to get back to the city and the comfort of her Beach Club bungalow and what on earth a man as wealthy as the sheikh was reputed to be was doing out here with this…this…this arrogant predator of a man!

'Oh, I think you'll find that anything concerning Xavier is very much my business,' came the gritted reply.

Something—Mariella wasn't sure what—must have alerted her to the truth. But she was too shocked by it to voice it, looking from his eyes to his mouth and then back again as she swallowed—hard—against the tight ball of shock tightening like ice around her heart. 'You…you…can't be the sheikh,' she told him defiantly, but her voice was trembling lightly, betraying her lack of confidence in her own denial.

Was this man her sister's lover…and Fleur's father? What was that sharp, bitter, dangerous feeling settling over her like a black cloud?

'You are the sheikh, aren't you?' she acknowledged bleakly.

A brief, sardonic inclination of his head was his only response but it was enough.

Turning away from him, she reached into the baby carrier and tenderly removed Fleur. Her whole face softened and illuminated with love as she hugged her and then kissed her before looking him straight in the eyes and saying fiercely to him, 'This is Fleur, the baby you have refused to both acknowledge and support.'

She had shocked him, Mariella realised, even though he had concealed his reaction very quickly.

As he stepped back from the vehicle for a second Mariella thought he was going to tell her to leave—and cravenly she wanted to do so! The man, the location, the situation were so not what she had been anticipating and prepared herself for. Each one of them in their different ways shattered not just her preconceptions but also her precious self-containment.

The man—try as she might she could just not envisage him in the club where Tanya had performed. The location made her ache for her painting equipment and brought her artistic senses to quick hunger. And her situation! Oh, no… Definitely no! This man had been her sister's lover, and was Fleur's father—

The shadowy fear that had stalked her adult years suddenly loomed terrifyingly sharply in front of her. She would not be like her mother; she would not ever allow herself to be vulnerable in any way to a man who could only damage her emotionally. The ability to fall in love with the wrong man might be learned, but it was not, to the best of Mariella's knowledge, inherited!

'Get out!'

Get out? With pleasure! Gripping the steering wheel, Mariella reached for the door, slamming it closed and then switching on the ignition at the same time, then she threw the vehicle into a furious spurt of reverse speed.

The tyres spun; sand filled the air. She could hear a thunderous banging on her driver's door as the car refused to budge. Looking out of the window, she saw Xavier looking at her in icy, furious disbelief.

Realising that she was bogged down in the swirling sand, Mariella switched off the engine. If he wanted her to leave he would have to move the vehicle for her, she recognised in angry humiliation.

As the engine died he was yanking the door open, demanding, 'What the hell do you think you are trying to do?'

'You told me to get out!' Mariella reminded him, equally angry.

'I meant get out of the car, not...' As he swore beneath his breath, to her shock he suddenly reached into the vehicle and snapped off her seat belt, grasping her so tightly around her waist that it actually hurt.

As he pulled her free of her seat and swung her to the ground she had a sudden shocking image of the two of them in her dream!

'Let go of me,' she demanded chokily, pushing him away. 'Don't touch me...'

'Don't touch you?'

Now that she was on the ground she realised just how far she had to look up to see the expression in his eyes.

'From what I've heard it isn't often those words leave your lips.'

Instinctively Mariella raised her hand, taking refuge in an act of female rebuttal and retaliation as ancient as the land around her, but immediately he seized her wrist in a punishing grip, his eyes glittering savagely as he curled his fingers tighter. 'Hell cat!' he taunted her mercilessly. 'One attempt to use your claws on me and, I promise you, you will regret it.'

'You can't go anywhere tonight,' he told her bluntly. 'There's a sandstorm forecast that would bury you alive before you could get even halfway back to the city. In your case it would be no loss, but for the sake of the child...'

The child...Fleur!

An agonised sound of distress choked in Mariella's throat. She could not stay here in this wilderness with this...this...savagely dangerous man, but her own common sense was telling her that she had no other option. Already the four-wheel drive was buried almost axle-deep in sand. She could taste it in her mouth, feel it on her skin. Inside the vehicle, Fleur had begun to cry again. Instinctively Mariella turned to go to her, but Xavier was there before her, lifting Fleur out.

The baby looked so tiny held in his arms. Mariella held her breath watching him... He was Fleur's father after all. Surely he must feel something? Some remorse, some guilt...something... True, he did pause to look at her, but the expression on his face was unreadable.

'She has your hair,' he told Mariella, before adding grimly, 'The wind is picking up. We need to get inside the tent. Where are you going?' he demanded as she turned back to the vehicle.

'I want to get Fleur's things,' she told him, tensing as he gave a sharp exclamation of irritation and overruled her.

'Leave them for now. I shall come back for them.'

Mariella couldn't believe how strong the wind had

become! The sand felt like a million tiny particles of glass shredding her skin.

By the time they reached the safety and protection of the pavilion, her leg muscles ached from the effort of fighting her way through the shifting sand.

Once inside the pavilion she realised that it was much larger than she had originally thought. A central area was furnished with rich carpets and low divans. Rugs were thrown over dark wood chests, and on the intricately carved tables stood oil lamps and candles. In their light Mariella could see two draped swags of cloth caught back in a dull gold rope as though they covered the entrance to two other inner rooms.

'Fleur needs something to eat, and a change of clothes,' she announced curtly, 'and I want to ring the Beach Club to tell them what has happened.'

'Use a telephone—in this intensity of sandstorm?' He laughed openly at her. 'You would be lucky to be able to use a landline, never mind a mobile. As for the child…'

'The child!' Mariella checked him bitterly. 'Even knowing the truth you still try to distance yourself from her, don't you? Well, let me tell you something—'

'No, let me tell you something… Any man could have fathered this child! I feel for her that she should have a mother of such low morals, a mother so willing to give herself to any and every man her eye alights on, but let me make it plain to you that I do not intend to be blackmailed into paying for a pleasure that was of so little value, never mind paying for a child who may or may not be the result of it!'

Mariella went white with shock and disbelief, but before she could defend her sister, Fleur started to cry in earnest.

Ignoring Xavier, Mariella soothed her, whispering tenderly. 'It's all right sweetheart, I know you're hungry...' Automatically as she talked to her Mariella stroked her and kissed the top of her head. She was so unbearably precious to her even though she was not her child. Being there at her birth had made Mariella feel as though they shared a very special bond, and awakened a maternal urge inside her she had not previously known she had.

'I don't know what she has to eat, but there is some fruit and milk in the fridge, and a blender,' he informed her.

Fridge? Blender? Mariella's eyes widened. 'You have electricity out here?'

Immediately he gave her a very male sardonic look.

'Not as such. There's a small generator, which provides enough for my needs.' He gave a brief shrug. 'After all, I come out here to work in peace...not to wear a hair shirt! The generator can provide enough warm water for you to bathe the child, although you, I am afraid, will have to share my bathing water.'

He was waiting for her to object, Mariella could see that. He was enjoying tormenting her.

'Since I shall only be here overnight, I dare say I can manage to forgo that particular pleasure,' she told him grittily.

'I shall go to your vehicle and bring the baby's things. You will find the kitchen area through that exit and to your right.'

Mariella had brought some dried baby food with her as well as some tinned food, which she knew would probably suit Fleur's baby digestion rather better than raw fruit, no matter how well blended! Even so, it would do no harm to explore their surroundings.

As she stepped through the opening she found that she was in a narrow corridor, on the right of which was an unexpectedly well equipped although very small kitchen, and, to the left, an immaculately clean chemical lavatory, along with a small shower unit.

The other opening off the main room must lead to a sleeping area, she decided as she walked back.

'What is all this stuff?' she heard Xavier demanding as he walked in with his arms full.

In other circumstances his obvious male lack of awareness of a small baby's needs might have been endearing, but right now...

Ignoring him and still holding Fleur, she opened the cool-bag in which she had placed her foods.

'Yummy, look at this, Fleur,' she murmured to her. 'Banana pudding...our favourite... Yum-yum.'

The look of serious consideration in Fleur's hazel eyes as she looked at her made her smile, and she forgot Xavier for a second as she concentrated on the baby.

'I suppose I shouldn't be surprised that she isn't receiving the nutrition of her mother's own milk,' she heard Xavier announcing critically.

Immediately Mariella swung round, her eyes dark with anger.

'Since her mother had to go back to work that wasn't possible!'

'How virtuous you make it sound, but isn't it the truth that the nature of that work—is anything but? But of course you will deny that, just as you will claim to know who the child's father is.'

'You are totally despicable,' Mariella stopped him. 'Fleur does not deserve to be treated like this. She is an innocent baby...'

'Indeed! At last we are in agreement about something. It is a pity, though, that you did not think of that before you came out here making accusations and claims.'

How could he be so cold? So unfeeling! According to the little Tanya had said about him, she had considered him to be a very emotional and passionate man.

No doubt in bed he was, Mariella found herself acknowledging. Her face suddenly burnt hotly as she recognised the unwanted significance of her private thoughts, and even worse the images they were mentally conjuring up for her; not with her sister as Xavier's partner—but herself!

What was happening to her? She was a cool-blooded woman who analysed, rationalised and resisted any kind of damaging behaviour to herself. And yet here she was...

'Just how long is this sandstorm going to last?' she asked abruptly.

The dark eyebrows rose. 'One day...two...three...'

'Three!' Mariella was aghast. Apart from the fact that Tanya would be beside herself if she could not get in touch with her, what was the prince going to think if he returned and she wasn't there?

'I have to feed and change Fleur.'

Luckily she had brought the baby bath with her as well as the changing mat, and Fleur's pram cum carry-cot, mainly because she had not been quite sure what facilities would be available at the oasis.

'Since it is obvious that you will have to stay the night, it is probably best that you and the child sleep in my... In the sleeping quarters,' Xavier corrected himself. Mariella's mouth went dry.

'And…where will you sleep?' she asked him apprehensively.

'In here, of course. When you have fed and bathed the child I suggest that we both have something to eat. And then—'

'Thank you, but I am perfectly capable of deciding for myself when I eat,' Mariella told him sharply.

She was far more independent, and a good deal more fiery, than he had anticipated, Xavier acknowledged broodingly when Mariella had disappeared with Fleur. And quite definitely not his younger cousin's normal type.

Thinking of Khalid made his mouth tighten a little. He had been both furious and disbelieving when Khalid had telephoned him to announce that he had fallen in love and was thinking of marrying a girl he had met in a dubious nightclub. Khalid had been in love before, but this was the first time he had considered marriage. At twenty-four Khalid was still very immature. When he married, in Xavier's opinion it needed to be someone strong enough to keep him grounded—and wealthy enough not to be marrying him for his money.

His frown deepened. It had been his cynical French grandmother who had warned him when he was very young that the great wealth he had inherited from his father would make him a target for greedy women. When he had been in his teens his grandmother had insisted that he spent time in France meeting the chic daughters of her own distant relatives, girls who in her opinion were deserving of inheriting the 'throne' his grandmother would have to abdicate when Xavier eventually married.

Well-born though they were, those girls had held

very little appeal for him, and, practical though he knew it would be, he found himself even less enamoured of the idea of contracting an arranged marriage.

Because of this he had already decided that it would be Khalid who would ultimately provide the heir to his enormous fortune and, more importantly, take his place as leader of their historically unique tribe. But he hadn't been in any hurry to nudge Khalid in the direction of a suitable bride—until he had learned of his plans *vis-à-vis* the impossible young woman who had forced her way into his private retreat!

He didn't know which of them had angered him the most! Khalid for his weakness in disappearing without leaving any indication of where he had gone, or the woman herself who had boldly followed up her pathetic attempt at blackmailing him via the letter she had sent Xavier, with a visit to his territory, along with the baby she was so determined to claim his cousin had fathered!

Physically he had not been able to see any hint in the child's features that she might be Khalid's; she was as prettily blonde as her mother, and as delicately feminine. The only difference was that, whilst her mother chose to affect those ridiculous, obviously false turquoise-coloured contact lenses, the baby's eyes were a warm hazel.

Like Khalid's?

There was no proof that the child was Khalid's, he reminded himself. And there was no way he was going to allow his cousin to marry her mother, without knowing for sure that Khalid was the father, especially now that he had actually met her. It was a wonder that Khalid had ever fallen so desperately in love with her in the first place!

'She has the grace of a gazelle,' he had written to him. 'The voice of an angel! She is the sweetest and most gentle of women...'

Well, Xavier begged to differ! At least on the two eulogising counts! Had he known when he had seen her at the airport just who she was he would have tried to find some way of having her deported there and then!

Remembering that occasion made him stride over to the opening to the pavilion, pulling back the cover to look outside. As had been forecast the wind was now a howling dervish of destruction, whipping up the sand so that already it was impossible to see even as far as the oasis itself. Which was a pity, because right now he could do with the refreshing swim he took each evening in the cool water of the oasis, rather than using the small shower next to the lavatory.

It both astounded and infuriated him that he could possibly want such a woman—she represented everything he most detested in the female sex: avarice, sexual laxity, selfishness—so far as he was concerned these were faults that could never be outweighed by a beautiful face or a sensual body. And he had to admit that, in that regard, his cousin had shown better taste than he had ever done previously!

Xavier allowed the flap of the tent to drop back in place and secured it. It irked him that Mariella should have the gall to approach him here of all places, where he came to retreat from the sometimes heavy burden of his responsibilities. A thin smile turned down the corners of his mouth. From what Khalid had described of the luxury-loving lifestyle they had shared, he doubted that she would enjoy being here. However little he cared about her discomfort, though there was the child to be considered.

The child! His mouth thinned a little more. Little Fleur was most definitely a complication he had not anticipated!

With Fleur fed, clean and dry, Mariella suddenly discovered just how tired she felt herself.

She had not expected Xavier to be pleased to be confronted with her accusations regarding his treatment of Tanya and Fleur, but the sheer savagery and cruelty with which he had verbally savaged her sister's morals had truly shocked her. This was after all a man who had very eagerly shared Tanya's bed, and who, even worse, had sworn that he loved her and that he wanted her to share a future with him!

In her opinion Tanya and Fleur were better off without him, just as she had been better off without the father who had deserted her!

Now that she had confronted him, though—and witnessed that he was incapable of feeling even the smallest shred of remorse—she longed to be able to get away from him, instead of being forced to remain here with him in the dangerous intimacy of this desert camp where the two of them...

Those ridiculous turquoise eyes looked even more theatrical and unreal in the pale triangle of her small exhausted face, Xavier decided angrily as he watched Mariella walking patiently up and down the living area of the pavilion whilst she rocked Fleur to sleep in her arms.

No doubt Khalid must have seen her a hundred or more times with her delicate skin free of make-up and those haunting, smudged shadows beneath her eyes as he lay over her in the soft shadows of the early morning, waking her with his caresses.

The fierce burst of anger that exploded inside him infuriated him. What was the matter with him? When he broke it down what was she after all? A petite, small-boned woman with a tousled head of strawberry-blonde hair that was probably dyed, coloured contact lenses to obscure the real colour of her eyes, skin the colour of milk and a body that had no doubt known more lovers than it was sensible for any sane-thinking adult to want to own to, especially one as fastidious in such matters as he was.

It would serve her right if he proved to Khalid just exactly what she was by bedding her himself! That would certainly ensure that his feckless cousin, who had abandoned his desk in their company headquarters without telling anyone where he was going or for how long, would, when he decided to return, realise just what a fate he had protected him from!

The child, though was a different matter. If she should indeed prove to be his cousin's, then her place was here in Zuran where she could be brought up to respect herself as a woman should, and to despise the greedy, immoral woman who had given birth to her!

CHAPTER THREE

MARIELLA woke up before Fleur had given her first distressed, hungry cry. She wriggled out from under the cool pure linen bedding to pad barefoot and naked to where she had placed the carry-cot.

Her khaki-coloured soft shape trousers could be re-worn without laundering, but the white cotton tee shirt she had worn beneath her jacket, and her underwear—no way.

Fastidiously wrinkling her nose at the very thought, Mariella had rinsed them out, deciding that even if they had not dried by morning wearing them slightly damp was preferable to putting them back on unwashed!

Picking Fleur up, she carried her back to the bed...Xavier's bed, a huge, low-lying monster of a bed, large enough to accommodate both a man and half his harem without any problem at all!

Sliding back beneath the linen sheets, Mariella stroked Fleur's soft cheek and watched her in the glow of the single lamp she had left on. She could tell from the way the baby sucked eagerly on her finger that she was hungry!

She had seen water in the fridge, and she had Fleur's formula. All she had to do was to brave the leopard's den in order to reach the kitchen!

And in order to do that she needed to find something to wear.

Whilst she was deciding between one of the pile of

soft towels Xavier had presented her with or the sheet itself, Fleur started to cry.

'Hush,' she soothed her gently. 'I know you're hungry, sweetheart…'

Xavier sighed as he heard Fleur crying. It was just gone two in the morning. The divan wasn't exactly the most comfortable thing to sleep on. Outside the wind shrieked like a hyena, testing the strength of the pavilion, but its traditional design had withstood many centuries of desert winds and Xavier had no fears of it being plucked away.

Throwing back the cover from his makeshift bed, he pulled on the soft loose robe and strode towards the kitchen, briskly removing one of the empty bottles Mariella had left in the sterilizer and mixing the formula.

His grandmother—an eccentric woman so far as many people were concerned—had sent him to work in a refugee camp for six months after his final year at school and before he went on to university.

'You know what it is to be proud,' she had told him when he had expressed his disdain for her decision. 'Now you need to learn what it is to be humble.

'Without humility it is impossible to be a great leader of men, Xavier,' she had informed him. 'You owe it to your grandfather's people to have greatness, for without it they will be swamped by this modern world and scattered like seeds in the wind.'

One of his tasks there had been to work in the crèche. For the rest of his life Xavier knew he would remember the emotions he had experienced at the sight of the children's emaciated little bodies.

Snapping the teat on the filled bottle, he headed for the bedroom.

The baby's cries were noticeably louder. Her feckless mother was no doubt sleeping selfishly through them, Xavier decided grimly, ignoring the fact that he himself had already noticed just how devoted Fleur's mother was to her.

Fleur was crying too much and too long to be merely hungry, Mariella thought anxiously as she caught the increasing note of misery in the baby's piercing cry.

To her relief, Fleur seemed to find some comfort as Mariella sat up in the bed and cuddled her against her own body.

'What's wrong, sweetheart?' she whispered to her. 'Are you missing your…?'

She froze as the protective curtain closing off the room swung open, snatching at the sheet to cover herself, her face hot with embarrassment as she glared at Xavier.

'What do you want?' she demanded aggressively.

'So you are awake. I thought—'

Fleur's eyes widened as she saw that he was carrying Fleur's bottle.

'What have you put in there?' Mariella demanded suspiciously, holding Fleur even tighter as he held the bottle out to her.

'Formula,' he told her curtly. 'What did you think was in it…hemlock? You've been reading too many idiotic trashy books!'

As she took the bottle from him and squirted a few drops onto the back of her hand, tasting it, he watched her.

'Satisfied?'

Looking fully at him, Mariella compressed her lips.

'My word,' she heard him breathe in disbelief. You even go to bed in those ridiculous coloured contact lenses! Hasn't anyone ever told you that no one actually has eyes that colour? So if it's your lovers you are hoping to impress and deceive...'

As Fleur seized eagerly on her bottle Mariella froze in outraged fury.

Coloured contact lenses. How dared he?

'Oh, is that a fact?' she breathed. 'Well, for your information, whether you consider it to be ridiculous or not this just happens to be the real colour of my eyes. I am not wearing contact lenses, and as for wanting to impress or deceive a lover—'

Fleur gave a wail of protest as in her agitation Mariella unwittingly removed the teat from her mouth. Apologising to the baby, and comforting her, Mariella breathed in sharply with resentment.

Real? The only thing about her that was real was her outrageous lying! Xavier decided lowering his lashes over his eyes as he discreetly studied the smooth swell of her breasts as her agitated movements dislodged the sheet.

No wonder she had not wanted to feed her child herself. With breasts so perfectly and beautifully formed she would be reluctant to spoil their shape. He could almost see the faint pink shadowing of the areolae of her nipples.

Uncomfortably he shifted his weight from one foot to the other, all too conscious of the effect she was having on him. She was doing it deliberately, he knew that... She was that kind of woman!

When he came here it was to withdraw from the fast-paced city life and concentrate on more cerebral matters, Xavier reminded himself sharply.

The sheet slipped a little farther.

Her flesh was creamy pale, untouched by the sun.

He frowned. Khalid had said specifically that he had
taken her to the South of France. Surely there she must
have exposed herself, as so many did, to the hot glare
of its sun and the ever hotter lustful looks of the men
who went there specifically to enjoy the sight of so
much young, naked flesh?

Knowing his cousin as he did, he couldn't imagine
that Khalid would be attracted to a woman too modest
to remove her bikini top!

He, on the other hand, found something profoundly
and intensely sensual about the thought of a woman
only revealing her bare breasts to her lover, her only
lover…

Worriedly Mariella studied Fleur's suddenly flushed
face, reaching out to touch her cheek. It burned beneath
the coolness of her own fingertips. Her heart jumped
with anxiety.

Xavier's stomach muscles clenched as she removed
her arm, revealing the full exposed curve of her breast.
As he had known it would be, her nipple was rose-pink
and so softly delicate that he ached to reach out and
touch it, explore its soft tenderness, feel it hardening
in eager demand beneath his caress.

In her anxiety for Fleur, Mariella had all but forgotten that he was there, only alerted to his sudden departure by the brief swirl of air eddying the door-
hanging as he left.

The minute he had gone Fleur started to cry again
and nothing Mariella could do would soothe her.

In the end, terrified that he would reappear at any
minute and demand that she silence the baby or else,
Mariella got out of the bed and, wrapping the sheet
around herself, started to pace the floor, gently rocking
Fleur as she did so.

To her relief after about ten minutes Fleur began to fall asleep. Gently carrying her back to her cot she started to lie her down, but the minute she did so the baby began to cry again.

Resolutely Mariella tried again…and again…and again…

Three hours later she finally admitted just how afraid she was. Fleur was crying pitifully now, her cheeks bright red and her whole body hot and sweaty. Mariella's own eyes ached and her arms were cramped with holding her as she walked up and down the bedroom.

Outside the wind still howled demoniacally.

'Oh, poor, poor baby,' Mariella whispered anxiously. Tanya had entrusted her precious child to her. How would she feel if she knew what Mariella had done? How she had brought her to the middle of the desert where there was no doctor and no way of getting to one? What if Fleur had something really seriously wrong with her? What if she had picked up some life-threatening infectious disease? What if…? Sick with anxiety and guilt, Mariella prayed that Fleur would be all right.

In the outer part of the pavilion Xavier could hear the fretful cry of the baby but he dared not go in to find out what was wrong. He could not trust himself to go in and find out what was wrong he admitted grimly.

An hour later, still trying to soothe and comfort Fleur, Mariella felt desperately afraid. It was obvious that Fleur wasn't well. The fear tormenting her could not be ignored any longer. Her hands trembling, Mariella relit all the oil lamps and then carefully undressed Fleur, slowly checking her for any sign of the rash that would confirm her worst fears and indicate that the baby could somehow have contracted meningitis.

Not content with having checked her skin once without finding any sign of a rash, Mariella did so again. When once again she could not find any sign of a rash, she didn't know whether to feel relieved or simply more anxious!

Tenderly wiping the tears from Fleur's hot face, she kissed her. Fleur grabbed hold of her finger and was trying to suck on it. No, not suck, Mariella realised— she was trying to bite on it. Fleur was cutting her first tooth!

All at once relief and recognition filled her. Fleur was teething—that was why she had been so uncomfortable. Mariella could well remember Tanya at the same age, her mother walking up and down with her as she tried to soothe her, explaining to Mariella just how much those sharp, pretty little teeth cutting through tender flesh hurt and upset the baby.

Naturally Mariella had tucked a good supply of paediatric paracetamol suspension into her baby bag before leaving home and, still holding Fleur, she went to get it.

'This will make you feel better, sweetheart,' she crooned, adding lovingly, 'And what a clever girl you are, aren't you, with your lovely new tooth? A very clever girl.'

Within minutes or so of the baby having her medicine, or so it seemed to a now totally exhausted Mariella, she was fast asleep. Patting her flushed face, Mariella smothered a yawn. Tucking Fleur into her cot, she made for her own bed.

Xavier frowned. It was well past daylight. He had showered and eaten his breakfast and switched on the laptop he had brought with him to do some work, but his mind wasn't really on it. Every time he thought about his cousin's mistress he was filled with unwanted and dangerous emotions. There hadn't been a sound from the bedroom in hours. No doubt working in a nightclub she was used to sleeping during the day… And very probably not on her own!

The very thought of the woman sleeping next door in his bed drove him to such an unfamiliar and furious level of hormone-fuelled rage that he could barely contain himself. And he was a man who was secretly proud of the fact that he was known for his fabled self-control!

Khalid should think himself very fortunate indeed that he had prevented him from marrying that turquoise-eyed seductress.

But Khalid did not think himself fortunate! Khalid thought himself very far from fortunate and had, in fact, left his cousin's presence swearing that he would not give up the woman he loved, no, not even if Xavier did try to carry out his threat and disinherit him!

His cousin was quite plainly besotted with the woman, and now that Xavier had met her for himself he was beginning to understand just how dangerous she was.

But not even Khalid's love would be strong enough to withstand the knowledge that she had been his cousin's lover. That she had given herself willingly to him! That the thought of ensnaring an even richer man than Khalid, in Xavier himself, had been enough to have her crawling into his bed.

That knowledge would hurt Khalid, but better that he was hurt quickly and cleanly now than that he spent a lifetime suffering a thousand humiliations at her hands! As he undoubtedly would do!

Surely the silence from the bedroom was unnatural. The woman should be awake by now, if only for the sake of her child!

Irritably Xavier strode towards the bedroom area, and pulled back the hanging.

Mariella was lying on the bed deeply asleep, one arm flung out, her pale skin gleaming in the soft light.

The thick strawberry-blonde hair was softly tousled, a few wisps sticking to her pink-cheeked face, lashes, which surely must be dyed to achieve that density of colour, surrounding the turquoise she insisted on claiming was natural.

In her sleep she sighed and frowned and made a little moue of distress before settling back into sleep.

Unable to drag his gaze from her, Xavier continued to watch her. There was nothing about what he knew of the type of person she was that could appeal to his aesthetic and cultured taste. But physically...

Physically, hormonally, she exerted such a pull over his senses that right now...

He had taken a step towards the bed without even realising it, the ache in his groin immediately a fierce, primal surge of white-hot need. If he took her in his arms and woke her now, would it be Khalid's name he heard on her lips?

That thought alone should have been enough to freeze his arousal to nothing, but instead he was filled with a savage explosion of angry emotion at the thought of any man's name on her lips that wasn't his own!

As he battled with the realisation of just what that

meant, his attention was suddenly distracted by the happy gurgling coming from the cot.

Striding over to it, he stared down at Fleur. Her child. The child another man had given her! A surge of primitive aching pain filled him.

Fleur had kicked off her blankets and was playing with her bare toes, smiling coquettishly up at him.

Xavier sucked in his breath. She was so small, so delicate…so very much like her mother.

Instinctively he bent to pick her up.

Mariella didn't know what woke her from her deep sleep, some ancient female instinct perhaps, she decided shakily as she stared across the room and saw Xavier bending over Fleur.

Gripping the bedclothes, she burst out frantically, 'Don't you dare hurt her.'

'Hurt her?' Tight-lipped, Xavier swung round. 'You dare to say that when she has already been hurt immeasurably simply by being brought into being as the child of a woman who…'

Unable to fully express his feelings, he compressed his mouth.

'I suppose she is used to being left to amuse herself whilst her mother sleeps off the effects of her night's work!'

Mariella could scarcely contain her fury.

'How dare you say such things, after the way you have behaved? You are the most loathsome, the most vile man I have ever met. You are totally lacking in any kind of compassion, or…or responsibility!'

Her eyes really were that colour, Xavier recognised in disbelief as he watched them darken from turquoise to inky blue-green.

Did they turn that colour when she was lost in passion? Was she as passionate in her sexual desire as she was in her anger? Of course she was…he knew that instinctively, just as he knew equally instinctively that if she were his…

'It is nearly eleven o' clock, the child must be hungry,' he told her tersely, infuriated by his own weakness in allowing such thoughts to creep into his head.

Eleven o'clock—how could it be? Mariella wondered guiltily, but a quick glance at her watch showed her that it was.

She couldn't wait to get back to the city and the sooner she and Fleur were on their way back there, the better, she decided as Xavier strode out of the room.

CHAPTER FOUR

MARIELLA frowned as she walked into the empty living area of the pavilion. Where was Xavier?

A laptop hummed quietly on a folding campaign table to one side of the pavilion. Xavier had obviously been working on it.

As she looked round the pavilion with its precious carpets and elegant few pieces of furniture, which she recognised as being expensively antique as well as functional, Mariella tried to imagine her dizzy half-sister in such a setting. Tanya was totally open about the fact that she was a girl who loved the bustle of cities, holidays in expensive, fashionable locations, modern apartments as opposed to traditional houses. Although she adored Fleur, self-indulgence was her by-word, and Mariella was finding it increasingly hard to visualise her sister ever being compatible with a man like Xavier, who she could not imagine truly sharing Tanya's tastes. He was too austere, surely. Too...

Tanya loved him, she reminded herself stubbornly, although she was finding that equally hard to imagine! He was just so totally not Tanya's type! Tanya liked happy-go-lucky, boyish, fun-loving men!

Fleur was sound asleep, and Mariella decided she would go outside to check on what was happening. She could no longer hear the sound of the wind battering against the walls of the pavilion, which hopefully meant that she would be able to make her way back to the city.

As she stepped outside she saw to her relief that the wind had indeed dropped. The air was now totally still and the sky had a dull ochre tinge to it. She could see her four-wheel drive, its sides covered in sand.

On the far side of the oasis, the rock face of the gorge rose steeply, its almost vertical face scarred here and there by the odd ledge.

There was a raw, elemental beauty about this hidden place, Mariella acknowledged, seeing it now with an artist's eye rather than the panicky apprehension of a lost traveller.

A scattering of palm trees fringed the water of the oasis, and beyond them lay a rough area of sparse, spiky grass. The rutted track she had driven down probably was a dried-out river bed, she could see now.

The quality of the stillness and the corresponding silence were almost hypnotic.

A movement on the other side of the oasis caught her eye, her body tensing as she recognised Xavier. He was dressed not in traditional robes, but in jeans and a tee shirt. He seemed to be checking the palm trees, she realised as he paused to inspect one before walking to another. He had obviously not seen her, but instinctively she drew farther back into the shadow cast by the pavilion.

He had turned away from the trees now and was staring across the oasis, shading his eyes as he looked up into the sky.

The storm hadn't weakened the roots of any of the palm trees, Xavier acknowledged. There was no reason why he shouldn't go back to the pavilion and continue with his work. And in fact pretty soon he would have to do so. Right now they were in the eye of the storm, but as soon as it moved on the wind would return with even greater force.

But he couldn't go back inside. Not whilst he was still visualising *her* lying on the bed...his bed...

Angrily he stripped off his tee shirt, quickly followed by the rest of his clothes. And began to wade out into the water.

Mariella couldn't move. Like someone deeply beneath the spell of an outside force she stood, muscles clenched, hardly daring to breathe as she fought to repel the sensation coiling through her, and shivering to each and every single sensitive nerve ending as her gaze absorbed the raw male beauty of Xavier's nudity.

As an artist she was fully aware of the complexities and the beauty of the human form, she had visited Florence and wandered lost in rapt awe as she studied the work of the great masters, but now she recognised she was seeing the work of the greatest Master of all.

Xavier was wading out into the water, the dull glaring sunlight glinting on flesh so warmly and evenly hued that it was immediately obvious that such nudity was normal for him.

As he moved through the water she could see the powerful sinews in his thighs contracting against its pressure. Trying to distract herself she visualised what lay inside that heavy satin male flesh, the bones, the muscles, the tissues, but instead of calming her down, it made her awareness of him increase, her wanton thoughts fiercely pushing aside the pallid academic images she was trying to conjure, in favour of some of their own: like a close-up of that sun-warmed flesh, roped with muscle, hard, sleek, rough with the same fine dark hair she could see so clearly arrowing down the centre of his body.

Only his buttocks were a slightly paler shade than the rest of his skin, taut and man-shaped, packed with the muscles that would drive…

Mariella shuddered violently, feeling as though she herself were sinking into a pool of sensation so deep and dangerous that she had no means of freeing herself from it.

Helplessly she watched as Xavier moved farther into the oasis until all she could see above the water were his head and shoulders. He ducked his whole body beneath the water and she held her breath, expelling it when she saw him break the surface several yards away, cleaving through it with long, powerful over-arm strokes that propelled him at a fierce and silent speed away from her.

She felt sick, shocked, furiously angry, terrifyingly vulnerable, aching from head to toe and most of all, deep down inside the most female part of her body, tormented by a need, a knowledge that ripped apart all her previous beliefs about herself.

She could not possibly want Xavier! But that…that merciless message her body had just given her could not be denied.

It sickened her to think of wanting a man who had hurt her sister so much; a man Tanya still loved so much. Such a feeling was a betrayal of everything within herself she most prided herself on. It was inconceivable that such a thing could be happening, just as it was inconceivable too that she, a woman who took such pride in her ability to mentally control the sexual and emotional side of her nature, could allow herself to feel so…so…

Dragging her gaze away from the oasis, Mariella closed her eyes.

Go on, admit it, she taunted herself mentally. You are so hungry for him that if he came to you now, you would let him do whatever he wanted with you right here and right now. Let him? You would urge him, encourage him, entice him...

Frantically Mariella shook her head, trying to shake away her own tormenting thoughts, the tormenting inner voice that was mocking her so openly.

Blindly she headed back for the pavilion, not seeing the hot breaths of wind tugging warningly at the topmost fronds of the palm trees, and not noticing, either, the bronze ring of light dulling the sun so menacingly.

Once inside the pavilion she hurried to check on Fleur who was still sleeping. She had only been outside for around half an hour, but it felt somehow as though she had passed through a whole time zone and entered another world. A world in which she no longer knew exactly who or what she was.

Quickly she started to get together their things. She didn't want to be here when Xavier came back. She couldn't bear to be here when he came back; she couldn't bear to face him, to be in the same room with him, the same space with him; in fact she wasn't sure right now if she could even bear to be in the same life with him.

She had never imagined that there could be anyone who could make her feel so threatened, so appalled by her own feelings, and so afraid of them. Flushed and sticky, she surveyed her uncharacteristically chaotic packing.

She would put their things in the four-wheel drive first, and then pop Fleur in and then she would drive back to the hotel and not stop until she got there.

Mariella took a deep breath. Once she was there she

would no doubt come to her senses and think of Xavier only as the man who had betrayed her sister, the man who was Fleur's father!

The wind was beginning to bend the palms as Mariella hurried out to the vehicle with their things, but she was oblivious to it as she wrestled with the heavy door and started to load the car.

Xavier saw her as he turned to swim another length. Treading water, he watched in furious disbelief as she struggled with the vehicle's door and then started to push the bulky container she had brought with her inside it.

There! Now all she had to do was go back for Fleur and then they could leave, hopefully whilst Xavier was too busy swimming to notice! And anyway, if he had wanted a swim that badly why couldn't he have worn…well, something? Why had he had to—to flaunt his undeniably supremely male and very, very sexy body in the way he had?

Engrossed in her thoughts, she failed to see Xavier wade out of the water and pull on his tee shirt and jeans without wasting time on anything else, before starting to run towards the pavilion into which she had already disappeared.

'Come on, my beautiful baby,' Mariella crooned lovingly to Fleur as she wrapped her up. 'You and I are going—'

'Nowhere!'

Turning round, white-faced and clutching Fleur protectively to her, Mariella glared at him. The fine cotton tee shirt was plastered to his very obviously still damp body and her skittering gaze slid helplessly downward to rest indiscreetly on the groin of his jeans at the same time as her heart came to rest against her chest wall in a massive breathtaking thud.

He was standing in the exit blocking her way, but infuriatingly, instead of registering this vitally important fact first, her senses seemed to be far too preoccupied with taking a personal inventory of the way he looked clothed and the way he had looked…before!

Reminding herself that she was an adult, mature businesswoman, well used to running her own life and making her own decisions, and not the sad female with her hormones running riot that she was currently doing a good impression of, she drew herself up to her full height and told him determinedly, 'I am taking Fleur back to the city and there is no way you are going to stop me. And anyway, I can't imagine why you would want us to stay after the way you have behaved! The things you have said!'

'Want you to stay? No, I don't!' Xavier confirmed harshly. 'But unfortunately you are going to have to, unless, of course, you want to condemn yourself and the baby to almost certain death.'

Mariella stared at him. What did he mean? Was he trying to threaten her? 'We're leaving,' she repeated, making for the exit, and trying to ignore both the furious thud of her heart and the fact that he was standing in the way.

'Are you mad? You'd be lucky to get above half a dozen miles before being buried in a sand drift. If you thought the wind coming here was bad, well, let me tell you that was nothing compared with what's blowing up out there now!'

Mariella took a deep breath.

'I've just been outside. There is no wind,' she told

him patiently, slowly spacing each word with immense care. 'The storm is over.'

'And you would know, of course, being an expert on desert weather conditions, no doubt. For your information, the reason that there was no wind, as you put it, is because we are, or rather we were in the eye of the storm. And anyone who knows anything about the desert would know that. Couldn't you feel the stillness? Didn't you notice the sand haze in the sky?' The look he shot her could have lit tinder at fifty paces, Mariella recognised shakily.

'You're lying,' she told him stubbornly, determined not to let him get the better of her. 'You just want to keep us here because—'

When she stopped he looked derisively at her.

'Yes. I want to keep you here because what?'

Because you know how dangerously much I want you, a treacherous little voice whispered insidiously inside Mariella's head, and you feel the same way.

Shuddering, she pushed her thoughts back into the realms of reality—and safety.

'You're lying,' she repeated doggedly, eyeing the exit rebelliously.

'Am I?' Moving to one side, he swept back the tent flap so that she could see outside.

The palms were bending so much beneath the strength of the wind that their fronds were brushing the sand.

As she stared in disbelief Mariella could hear the strength of the wind increasing until it whistled eerily around the oasis, physically hurting her ears.

Out of nowhere it whipped up huge spirals of sand, making them dance in front of her. She could hardly

see the sun or differentiate any longer between sand
and sky.

Disbelievingly she took a step outside and cried out
in shock as she was almost lifted off her feet when the
wind punched into her. In her arms, Fleur screamed
and was immediately removed to the protection of a
much stronger and safer pair as Xavier snatched Fleur
from her.

The thought of what would have happened to them
if they had been caught in the open desert in such conditions drove the colour from Mariella's face.

'Now do you believe me?' Xavier demanded grimly
when they were both back inside and he had secured
the tent flap.

Reaching out to take Fleur from him, Mariella,
whose fingers had inadvertently come into contact with
the damp heat of his tee-shirt-clad chest, withdrew her
hand so fast she almost lost her balance.

Immediately Xavier gripped her arm to steady her,
supporting whilst he did so, so that it looked almost as
though he were embracing them both, holding them
both safe.

Against all rationality, given what she knew about
him, Mariella discovered that her eyes were burning
with emotional tears. She should be crying, she acknowledged grimly, for her own stupidity in allowing
her emotions to be aroused so much for so little real
reason! Pulling back from him, she demanded, 'Just
how long is this storm going to last?'

'At least twenty-four hours, perhaps longer. Since
the storm is making it impossible to receive any kind
of communication signal, it is impossible to know.

Such storms are rare at this time of year, but when they do occur they are both unpredictable and fierce.'

As was Xavier himself, Mariella decided as she took Fleur from him.

CHAPTER FIVE

GETTING up from the bed where she had been lying reading one of the research books she had brought to Zuran with her, Mariella went to check on Fleur.

A brief glance at her watch showed her that it was nearly eight p.m. Fleur was awake but obviously quite content, and happy to oblige when Mariella checked her mouth to look at the small pearly white tooth just beginning to appear. Her face was still a little bit swollen and flushed, but the paracetamol seemed to have eased the pain she had suffered the previous night.

Mariella had retreated to 'her bedroom' late in the afternoon, desperate to escape from the highly charged atmosphere in the main living area.

It had become impossible for her to look at Xavier without imagining him as he had been earlier: naked...male.

He had retrieved the things she had carried out to the four-wheel drive and put them back in the bedroom, and when Mariella had come across a sketch-book and pencils she had forgotten she had brought, along with her book, she had fallen on the book with a surge of relief.

Apart from the fact that she genuinely found the subject interesting, it gave her a perfect excuse to distance herself from Xavier, who had been busily working on his laptop.

On the pretext of Fleur needing a nap she had come

into the sleeping quarters and had remained there ever since.

A thorough understanding of anatomy was essential for any painter in her type of field, and she had quickly become totally engrossed in trying to trace the development of the modern-day racehorse from the original Arabian bloodstock.

As Kate had said, the potential commission from the prince was indeed a prestigious one.

Picking up her sketch-book, Mariella started to work. Those incredible muscles that powered every movement... Her pencil flew over the paper, her absorption in what she was doing only broken when Fleur started to demand her attention.

Smiling, she discarded the sketch-book and then frowned sharply as she looked at what she had done, her face burning mortified and disbelieving scarlet.

How on earth had that happened? How on earth had she managed to sketch, not a horse, but a man... Xavier...Xavier, swimming, Xavier standing, Xavier: his body lean and naked, clean-muscled and powerful.

Guiltily, Mariella flipped over the page. Fleur was blowing kisses at her and becoming increasingly vociferous.

Tucking the sketch-pad safely out of sight, Mariella went to her and picked her up, fastening her into her car seat and then carrying her into the kitchen.

'Look at this yummy dinner you're going to have,' Mariella crooned to Fleur as she prepared her food.

It had been her intention to take Fleur back into the bedroom to feed her, but instead Mariella carried her into the living area.

Fleur was Xavier's daughter, after all, and perhaps

they both needed reminding just what that meant, albeit
for very different reasons! Perhaps too he ought to be
made to see just what he was missing out on by not
acknowledging her.

He was working on the laptop when Mariella walked
in and put Fleur down in her seat so that she could feed
her.

She was a strong, healthy baby with a good appetite,
who thankfully no longer seemed to be too bothered
by the tooth she had been cutting.

Absorbed in her own enjoyable task, Mariella didn't
realise that Xavier had stopped work to turn and study
them until some sixth sense warned her that they were
being watched.

His abrupt, 'She has your nose,' made Mariella's
hand tremble slightly. She and Tanya shared the same
shaped nose, which they had both inherited from their
mother. Fleur had their nose, but, according to Tanya,
her father's deliciously long thick eyelashes.

Mariella could feel her face starting to burn. What
was it about a certain type of man that enabled him to
behave so uncaringly towards the child he had fathered?

The way Xavier was behaving towards Fleur was so
reminiscent of the way her father had behaved towards
her! She knew all too well what it was like to grow up
feeling rejected and unloved by one's father and she
couldn't bear to see that happen to Fleur!

Xavier ought to be made to see that she was at least
in part his responsibility instead of being allowed to
just walk away from her. The way she felt had nothing
whatsoever to do with money, Mariella recognised, and
everything to do with emotion.

Fleur had finished her meal and was beginning to

drift off to sleep. Bending down to double check that she was comfortably fastened into her seat, Mariella tenderly kissed her downy cheek, then straightened up and headed for the kitchen to wash out her feeding things.

Left on his own with Fleur, Xavier studied her frowningly. She was far fairer skinned than his cousin and, whilst Xavier could see an unmistakable physical resemblance to Mariella in her, he could see none to Khalid. Fast asleep now, Fleur gave a small quiver.

Immediately Xavier went over to her. Desert nights could be unbelievably cold—she felt warm enough, but perhaps she needed an extra cover?

He could hear Mariella in the kitchen and so he went through into the bedroom area, to get an extra blanket from the carry-cot.

Mariella had tucked her sketch-pad in between the carry-cot and the box of baby equipment, and as Xavier reached for a blanket he saw the sketch-pad, and its very recognisable sketches.

Frowning, he picked it up and studied it.

Having washed Fleur's feeding cup, Mariella walked into the bedroom intending to put it away, coming to an abrupt halt as she saw Xavier bending towards the carry-cot.

'Where is Fleur?' she demanded immediately. 'What—?'

'She's fast asleep where you left her,' Xavier answered her adding, 'From looking at her, it is plain to see her resemblance to you, but as to there being a similarity to her supposed father...'

Mariella had had enough.

'How can you deny your own flesh and blood?' she

demanded bitterly. 'I can't imagine how *any* woman could ever desire you, never mind—'

Before she could say 'Tanya' he had cut her off as he asked with cutting brutality, 'Indeed? Then, what may I ask, are these?'

Mariella felt the breath wheeze from her lungs like air squeezed from a pair of bellows as he held up in front of her her own sketches.

Chagrin, embarrassment, guilt and anger fused into one burning, searing jolt of emotional intensity had her lunging frantically towards him, intent on snatching her betraying sketches from him. But Xavier was withholding them from her, holding them out of her reach with one hand whilst he fended her attempt to repossess them with the other.

Furiously Mariella redoubled her efforts, flinging herself at him, and trying to shake off his hard grip of her wrist as she did so.

'Give those back to me. They are mine,' she insisted breathlessly.

As she tried to reach up for them she overbalanced slightly, her fingers curling into his arm, her fingernails accidentally raising livid weals on his olive skin.

'Why, you little...'

Shocked as much by her own inadvertent action as his reaction to it, Mariella went stiff with disbelief as he suddenly dropped the sketches and grabbed hold of her waist with both hands.

'Other men might have been willing to let you get away with such behaviour, but I most certainly do not intend to!' she could hear Xavier grating at her as he gave her a small, angry shake.

Mariella could feel the edge of the bed behind her as she turned and twisted, frantically trying to break free, but Xavier was refusing to let her go and suddenly she was lying on the bed, with Xavier arching over her, pinning her down.

He was angry with her, Mariella recognised as she stared into the lava-grey heat of his eyes, but her senses were telling her something else as well and a savage little quiver then ran unmistakably through her own body as she realised that something else had nothing whatsoever to do with fear.

Xavier wanted her! Mariella could sense, feel it, breathe it in the sudden tension that filled the air, engulfing, locking them both in a place out of time.

This was fate, Xavier decided recklessly, a golden opportunity given to him to prove to his cousin beyond any shadow of a doubt that this woman was not worthy of his love, but, strangely, as he lowered his mouth to Mariella's it wasn't his duty towards his cousin that was filling his thoughts, driving him with an intense ferocity that a part of him recognised was more dangerous than anything he had previously experienced.

This was wrong, desperately wrong, the very worst kind of betrayal, Mariella acknowledged as her whole body was savaged by a mixture of anguish and hunger.

Xavier's mouth burned hers, its possession every bit as harsh and demanding as she had expected, barely cloaking a hunger that scorched right through her body to her fingertips.

Helplessly her mouth responded to the savage demand of his, her body quivering as his tongue probed her closed lips demanding entry. Somehow, some time she had lifted her hands to his body so that she was gripping his shoulders. To push him away, or to draw him closer?

His teeth tugged ruthlessly at her bottom lip and her

resistance ebbed away, like the inner tears of shame
and guilt she was silently crying inside for her inability
to resist giving in to flames of her own desire as they
licked and darted inside her, burning down her pathet-
ically weak defences. Without knowing how she knew,
she knew that this man, this moment was something a
part of her had been waiting for, for a very long time.
Even the merciless intent of his sensual need was
something that a part of her was fiercely responsive to.

Her eyes, magnificent in their emotional intensity,
shimmered from turquoise to dark blue-green. Xavier
was mesmerised by them, caught in their brilliance.
How could such cool colours glow so hotly? But not
nearly so hotly as his own body.

Without knowing what she was doing, Mariella
raked the taut flesh of his arm—deliberately this time—
her body galvanised by deep, urgent shudders as his
kiss possessed her mouth, his tongue thrusting into its
warm softness.

Mariella tried to deny what she was feeling, pulling
frantically away from Xavier, in a desperate attempt to
escape and to save them both from the very worst kind
of betrayal, but having shared her surrender Xavier refused to let her go, pinning her to the bed with the
weight of his body hot and heavy on hers, making her
melt, making her ache, making her writhe in helpless
supplication and moan into his mouth, a tiny keening
sound lost beneath the greater sounds of their bodies
moving on the bed. The rustle and rasp of fabric against
flesh, of two people both revealing their hunger in the
accelerated sound of their breathing, and the frantic
thud of their heartbeats.

Xavier's mouth grazed her skin, exploring the curve
of her jaw, the soft vulnerability of her throat as she

automatically arched her whole body. The hot, fevered feel of his mouth against her flesh made her arch even more, shuddering in agonised pleasure.

Just a few kisses, that was all it was… And yet she felt as possessed by him, as aching for him as though he had touched her far more intimately and for far, far longer. The desire she was feeling was so acute, so very nearly unbearable, that Mariella dared not allow herself to imagine how she was going to feel when he did touch her more intimately. And yet at the same time she knew that if he didn't—

When his hand covered her breast she cried out, unable to stop herself, and felt his responding groan shudder through his body. She could hear herself making small, whimpering sounds of distress as she tugged at his clothes, her own body consumed by a need to be completely bare to his touch, to be open to him…

And yet when he had finally removed them and she was naked, a sense of panic that was wholly primitive and instinctive ripped through her, causing her to go to cover her naked breasts protectively with her own hands. But Xavier was too quick for her, his fingers snapping round her wrists, pinioning her hands either side of her head as he knelt over her.

Mariella felt the heavy thread of her own hungry desire. She just had time to see the molten glitter of Xavier's answering hunger before he looked down at her exposed breasts. A sinful desire slid hotly through her veins, her face burning as she watched him absorbing the taut swell of her breasts as her nipples tightened and darkened, openly inciting the need she could hear and feel in his indrawn breath, even before he lowered his head to her body.

The feeling of him slowly circling first one and then

the other nipple with the moist heat of his tongue, whilst she lay powerless beneath him, should surely have inflamed her angry independence instead of sending such a sheet of white-hot sensuality pouring through her that her belly automatically concaved under its pressure whilst her sex ached and swelled.

Mariella closed her eyes. Behind her closed eyelids she could see him as she had done in the oasis, just as she wanted to see him again now, she recognised as her body began to shudder. Slow, deep, galvanic surges of desire that ripped rhythmically through her, her body moving to the suckle of his mouth against her breast.

She could feel his knee parting her thighs her body already aching for the aroused feel of him, hot, heavy, masculine as he urgently moved against her.

He was losing himself, drowning in the way she was making him feel, his self-control in danger of being burned away to nothing. Just the sight of her swollen breasts, their nipples tight and aroused from his laving of them, made him ache to possess her, to complete and fill her, to complete himself within her.

The moment Xavier released her wrists, Mariella tugged impatiently at his clothes, answering her demanding need for him. Immediately Xavier helped her, guiding her hands over buttons and zips and then flesh itself as she moaned her pleasure against the hot skin of his throat when her fingertips finally tangled with the soft, silky hair she had ached to touch earlier.

His body, packed hard with muscle, was excitingly alien and overpoweringly male. His impatience to be a part of her made her gasp and shudder as he kissed her throat, her shoulder and then her mouth, whilst he wrapped her tightly in his arms so that they were lying intimately, naked body to naked body.

The feel of him pressing against her. Hot and hard, aroused, his movement against her urgently explicit, was more than she could withstand.

Eagerly she coiled herself around him, opening herself to him, crying out as she felt him enter her, each movement powerful and sure, strong and urgent.

Already her own body was responding to his movement, her muscles clinging to him. Sensually stroking him and savouring each thrust, she could feel him strengthening inside her, filling her to completion, picking up the rhythm of her body and carrying…driving them both with it.

'Never mind the child he has given you, has my cousin given you this? Has he made you feel like this when he holds you? When he possesses you? When he loves you? Was *this* how it was between you when you made Fleur together?'

Mariella's whole body stiffened.

'Did you give yourself to him as easily as you did to me? And how many others have there been?'

With a fierce cry, she pulled away from him, her brain barely able to take in what he was saying, her body and emotions in such deep shock that removing herself from him made her feel as though she were physically dying.

The shock of her rejection tore at Xavier's guts. He wanted to drag her back into his arms, where surely she belonged, to roll her into the bed beneath him and to fill her with himself, to make her admit that no other man had ever or could ever give her or share with her what he could. But most of all he wanted to fill her with the life force that would ultimately be his child.

A part of him recognised that there was no more elemental drive than this, to fill a woman's body with
one's child in order to drive out her commitment to
another man and the child he had already given her.
The barbaric intensity of his own emotions shocked
him. He had done what he had done for Khalid's sake,
to protect him, he reminded himself, and to reinforce
that fact he told her, 'It's a little too late for that now!
You have already proved to me just what you are, and
once Khalid learns how willing you were to give yourself to me he will quickly realise how right I was to
counsel him against you.'

He had taken her to bed for that? Because of that?
So that he could denounce her to another man?

In the outer room Fleur suddenly started to cry.
Dragging on her clothes, Mariella hurried in to her,
picking her up and holding her tightly as though just
holding her could somehow staunch the huge wound
inside her that was haemorrhaging her life force. She
was shaking from head to foot with reaction, both from
what had happened and from what she had just learned.

Fleur was not Xavier's child! Xavier's cousin was
Fleur's father! But Xavier believed that she was Fleur's
mother. And because of that he had taken her to bed,
out of a cold-hearted, despicable, damnable desire to
prove to his cousin that she was a...a wanton who
would give herself to any man!

Fate had been doubly kind to her, she told herself
staunchly: firstly in ensuring that she had not betrayed
her sister, and secondly in giving her incontrovertible
proof of just what manner of man Xavier was!

CHAPTER SIX

As SHE stepped inside the welcome familiarity of her Beach Club bungalow, Mariella allowed herself to expel a shaky sigh of relief. Her first since she had left the oasis!

Now that she was safely here, perhaps she could allow herself to put the events of the last forty-eight hours firmly behind her. Lock them away in a very deep sealed drawer marked, 'Forget for ever.'

But how could she forget, how could any human being forget an act as deliberately and cold-bloodedly cruel and damaging as the one Xavier had perpetrated against her?

If she herself had been a different kind of woman she might have taken a grim sense of distorted pleasure in knowing that, for all he might try to deny it, Xavier had physically wanted her. In knowing it and in throwing that knowledge back at him! Instinctively she knew that he would be humiliated by it, and if any man deserved to be humiliated it was Xavier!

Just thinking about him was enough to have Mariella's hands curling into small, passionately angry fists. As her heart drove against her ribs in sledgehammer blows. How could he possibly not have recognised that she would never, ever, ever under any circumstances betray her love, and that if she had been another man's lover nothing he could have done would have tempted her to want him? Hadn't her body itself proclaimed to him the unlikeliness, the impossibility of her being Fleur's mother and any man's intimate lover?

But believing that he had been Tanya's lover hadn't stopped her, had it?

She would carry that shame and guilt with her to her deathbed, Mariella acknowledged.

The message light on the bungalow's communications system was flashing, indicating that she had received several telephone calls, all from the prince's personal assistant, she discovered when she went to check them. Before answering them, the first thing she intended to do now that she was safely back at the hotel was ring her sister and double check that she had not misunderstood Xavier—he was not Tanya's lover or Fleur's father!

And once she had that confirmation safely in her possession, then Xavier would be history!

It took her several attempts to get through to Tanya, who eventually answered the phone sounding breathless and flustered.

'I'm sorry, Ella,' she apologised quickly. 'But things are really hectic here and... Look, I can't really talk right now. Is Fleur okay?'

'Fleur is fine. She's cut her first tooth, but, Tanya, there's something I've got to know,' Mariella told her, firmly overriding her attempts to end the call.

'I must know Fleur's father's name, Tanya. It's desperately important!'

'Why? What's happened? Ella, I can't tell you...'

Hearing the panic in her sister's voice, Mariella took a deep breath. 'All right! But if you won't tell me who he is, Tanya, then please at least tell me that his first name isn't Xavier...'

'Who?' Tanya's outraged shriek almost hurt her eardrums. 'Xavier? You mean that horrid cousin of Khalid's? Of course he isn't Fleur's father. I hate him... He's the one responsible for parting me and Khalid! He sent Khalid away! He doesn't think that I'm good enough for him! Anyway...how do you know about Xavier, Ella? He's an arrogant, overbearing, old-fashioned, moralistic beast, who lives in the Dark Ages! Look, Ella, I've got to go... Love to Fleur and lots of kisses.'

She ended the call before Mariella could stop her, leaving her gripping the receiver tensely.

But at least she had confirmed that Xavier was not Fleur's father.

Determinedly Mariella made herself turn her attention to her messages.

The prince had now returned to Zuran and wanted her to get in touch with his personal assistant.

'Don't worry,' the prince's personal assistant reassured Mariella when she rang him a few minutes later to explain why she had not returned his calls.

'It is just that the prince is hosting a charity breakfast tomorrow morning at the stables and he wanted to invite you as his guest. His Highness is very enthusiastic about his project of having the horses painted, but of course this is something you will be having formal discussions with him about at a later date. The breakfast is a prestigious dressy event, although we do ask all our guests not to wear strong perfumes, as this can affect the horses.'

'It sounds wonderful,' Mariella responded. 'However, there is one small problem. I have brought my four-month-old niece to Zuran with me, as the prince knows. I am looking after her for my sister, and—'

'That is no problem at all,' the PA came back promptly. 'Crèche facilities are being provided with fully trained nannies in attendance. A car will be sent to collect both you and the baby, of course.'

Mariella had previously attended several glitzy society events at the invitation of her clients, including one particularly elegant trip to France for their main race of the season at Longchamps—a gift from a client, which she had repaid with a 'surprise' sketch of his four-year-old daughter on her pony, and, recalling the sophistication and glamour of the outfits worn by the Middle Eastern contingent on that occasion, she suspected that she was going to have to go shopping.

Two hours later, sitting sipping coffee in the exclusive Zuran Designer Shopping Centre, Mariella smiled ruefully to herself as she contemplated her assorted collection of shiny shopping bags.

The largest one bore the name, not of some famous designer, but of an exclusive babywear store. Unable to choose between two equally delicious little outfits for Fleur, Mariella had ended up buying her niece both.

She had been rather less indulgent on her own account, opting only to buy a hat—an outrageously feminine and eye-catching model hat, mind you!—a pair of ridiculously spindly heeled but totally irresistible sandals, which just happened to be the exact shade of turquoise-blue of the silk dress she had decided to wear to the charity breakfast, and a handbag in the same colour, which quite incredibly had the design of a galloping horse picked out on it in sequins and beads.

And best of all she had managed not to think about

Xavier at all…well, almost not at all! And when she had thought about him it had been to reiterate to herself just what a total pig he was, and how lucky she was that all she had done was give in to a now unthinkable and totally out of character, momentary madness, which would never, ever be repeated. After all, there was no danger of her ever allowing herself to become emotionally vulnerable to any man—not with her father's behaviour to remind her of the danger of falling in love—never mind a man who had condemned himself in the way that Xavier had!

Having drunk her coffee, she gathered up her bags and checked that Fleur was strapped securely in her buggy before heading for the taxi rank.

It had been a long day. She had hardly slept the night before, lying awake in Xavier's bed, her thoughts and her emotions churning. And then there had been the long drive back to Zuran this morning after her prayers had been answered and the storm had died away.

True, she had had a brief nap earlier, but now, even though it was barely eight in the evening, she was already yawning.

Xavier paced the floor of the pavilion. He should, he knew, be rejoicing in his solitude and the fact that that woman had gone! And of course he would have no compunction whatsoever in telling Khalid just how easily and quickly she had betrayed the 'love' she had claimed to have for him!

That ache he could feel in his body right now meant nothing and would very quickly be banished!

But what if Khalid refused to listen to him? What if, despite everything he, Xavier, had said to him, he insisted on continuing his relationship with her?

If Fleur was Khalid's child then it was only right that he should provide for her. Xavier tried to imagine how he would feel if Khalid were to set his mistress and their child up in a home in Zuran. How he would feel knowing that Khalid was living with her, sharing that home...sharing her bed?

Angrily he strode outside. Even the damned air inside the tent was poisoned by her perfume—that and the scent of baby powder! He would instruct his staff to dispose of the bedding and replace it with new, just in case her scent might somehow manage to linger and remind him of an incident he now wanted to totally forget!

But even outside he was still haunted by his mental images of her. Her ridiculous turquoise eyes, her creamy pale skin, her delicate bone structure, her extraordinarily passionate response to him that had driven him wild, driven him over the edge of his control to a place he had never been before. The sweet, hot, tight feel of her inside, as though she had never had another lover, never mind a child! No wonder poor, easygoing Khalid had become so ensnared by her!

Fleur was certainly attracting a lot of attention, Mariella reflected tenderly as people turned to look at the baby she was carrying in her arms, oblivious to the fact that it was her own appearance that was attracting second looks from so many members of the fashionably dressed crowd already filling the stable yard.

Her slim silk dress had originally been bought for a friend's wedding, its soft, swirling pattern in colours that ranged from palest aqua right through to turquoise. Over it, to cover her bare arms, Mariella was wearing a toning, velvet-edged, silk-knit cardigan, several shades paler than her hat and shoes.

A member of the prince's staff had been on hand to greet her as she stepped out of the limousine that had been sent to collect her, and to pass her on to a charming young man, who was now taking her to introduce her to the prince.

The purpose-built stables were immaculate, the equine occupants of the stalls arching their long necks and doing a good deal of scene stealing, as though intent on making the point that they were the real stars of the event and not the humans who were invading their territory.

The breakfast was to be served in ornamental pavilioned areas, off which was the crèche, so Mariella had been informed.

Her stomach muscles tightened a little as she saw the group of people up ahead of her. People of consequence and standing, no matter how they were dressed, all possessed that same air of confidence, Mariella acknowledged as the crowd opened up and the man at the centre of it turned to look at her.

'Miss Sutton, this is his Royal Highness,' her young escort introduced her to the prince, her potential client.

'Miss Sutton!' His voice was warm, but Mariella was aware of the sharp, assessing look he gave her.

'Your Highness,' she responded, with a small inclination of her head.

'I have been very impressed with your work, Miss Sutton, although I have to say that, especially in the case of my friend and rival Sir John Feinnes, you have erred on the side of generosity in the stature and muscle you have given his ''Oracle''.'

A small smile dimpled Mariella's mouth.

'I simply reflect what I see as an artist, Highness,' she told him demurely.

'Indeed. Then wait until you have seen my animals. They are the result of a breeding programme that has taken many years' hard work, and I want them to be painted in a way that pays full tribute to their magnificence.'

And to his own, Mariella decided, but tactfully did not say so.

'My friend Sir John also tells me that you have some very innovative ideas... The finishing touches are currently being put to an exclusive enclosure at our racecourse, which will bear my family name, and it occurs to me that there could be an opportunity there for...' He paused.

Mariella suggested, tongue in cheek, 'Something innovative?'

'Indeed,' he agreed. 'But this is not a time to discuss business. I have invited you here as my guest, so that you can meet some of your subjects informally, so to speak...'

Fleur, who had been staring around in wide-eyed silence, suddenly turned her head and smiled at him.

'You have a beautiful child,' he complimented her.

'She is my niece,' Mariella informed him. 'I am looking after her for my sister. I think my agent did explain.'

'Yes. I am sure she did! I seem to remember that my personal assistant did mention the little one.'

Some new guests were waiting to be presented to him, and Mariella stepped discreetly to one side. In the distance on the racecourse she could see a string of horses being exercised, whilst here in the yard there were grooms and stable hands all wearing khaki shorts or trousers, and tee shirts in one of the prince's three racing colours denoting their status within the hierarchy of the stables.

'If you would care to take the baby to the crèche,' the prince's assistant was asking politely.

Firmly Mariella shook her head. Such was her sense of responsibility towards her niece that she preferred to keep her with her for as long as she could, and, besides, the yard was far too busy for her to be able to do even the briefest of preliminary sketches of the animals. The event was providing her with a wonderful opportunity to do some people watching, though.

Surveying the crowd filling the prince's racing yard, Xavier wondered what on earth he was doing here. This kind of social event was normally something he avoided like the plague! It was much more Khalid's style than his, and if Khalid had not taken leave of absence without warning he would have been the one to attend the event! However, since Xavier was involved in shared business interests with the prince, he had felt that perhaps he should attend the breakfast—especially as it was in aid of a charity that he fully supported.

Several people had already stopped him to talk with him, including various members of the royal family, but he now felt that he had done his duty and was on the point of leaving when he suddenly frowned as he caught sight of a silky flash of turquoise-blue as the crowd in front of him momentarily parted.

Grimly he started to stride towards it.

People were starting to move towards the pavilioned area where the breakfast was about to be served, but Mariella hesitated a little uncertainly, suspecting that it would be a diplomatic move now to take Fleur over to the crèche area rather than into the pavilions. A little uncertainly she glanced round, unsure as to what to do, and hoping that she might see the prince's helpful assistant.

Xavier saw Mariella before she saw him, his eyebrows snapping together in seething fury as he realised his suspicions had been confirmed. It was her! And he had no difficulty in guessing just what she was doing here! Some of the richest men in Zuran were here, and very few of them were unlikely to at least be tempted by the sight of her! From the top of the confection of straw and tulle she was wearing on top of her head to the tip of the dainty little pink-painted toenails revealed by shoes so fragile that he was surprised that she dared risk wearing them, especially when carrying her child, she looked a picture of innocent vulnerability. But of course she was no such thing! And dressing the baby in an outfit obviously chosen to match hers seemed to proclaim their mother and baby status to the world.

Unaware of the fact that Nemesis and all the Furies were about to bear down on her with grim zeal in the shape of a very angry and disapproving male, Mariella shifted Fleur's weight in her arm.

'Very fetching! Trust you to be here, and with the very latest European accessory—I have to tell you, though, that you've misjudged its effect in Zuran!'

'Xavier!' Mariella felt her legs wobble treacherously in her high heels as she stared at him in shock.

'I don't know how you managed to get past the security staff—although I suspect I can guess how!' he told her cynically. 'Kept women and those who sell their favours to the highest bidder are normally kept out of such events.'

Kept women! His condemnation stung not just her pride, but her sense of sisterly protection for Tanya. She knew that if this conversation were to continue, she would have to explain she was not Fleur's mother, but right now she was due in the pavilion for breakfast. She was here on business and she would not jeopardise the commission by having an argument with Xavier in front of the prince! 'I refuse to speak with you if you are going to be so rude,' she said tersely. 'Now, if you'll excuse me, I must go and join the others.' A flash of light to her left made her gasp as she realised a photographer had just caught the two of them on camera!

'Don't think I don't know what you're doing here,' Xavier told her challengingly. 'You know that Khalid is going to come to his senses and realise just what you are, and you're looking for someone to take his place, and finance you.'

'Finance her!' The feathers nestling in the swathes of chiffon on Mariella's hat trembled as she shook with outrage.

'For your information, I do not need anyone to finance me, as you put it. I am completely financially independent.' As she saw his expression Mariella turned on her heel.

Hurrying away from him, she tensed as she suddenly felt a touch on her arm, but when she looked round it was only the prince's assistant.

'The Prince would like you to join his table for breakfast, Miss Sutton.' he told her. 'If I may escort you first to the crèche,' he added tactfully.

Angrily Xavier watched as the crowd swallowed her up. How dared she lie to him and claim to be financially independent, especially when she knew he knew the truth about her?

She was the most scheming and deceitful woman he had ever met, a woman he was a total fool to spare the smallest thought for!

The conversation around the breakfast table was certainly very cosmopolitan, Mariella decided as she listened to two other women discussing the world's best spa resorts, whilst the men debated the various merits of differing bloodstock.

After the breakfast was over and people were beginning to drift away, the prince came over to Mariella.

'My assistant will telephone you to make formal arrangements for us to discuss my commission,' he told her.

'I was wondering if it would be possible for me to visit your new enclosure?' Mariella asked him. 'Or, failing that, perhaps see some plans?'

She had the beginnings of a vague idea which, if the prince approved, would be innovative, but first she needed to see the enclosure to see if it would work.

'Certainly. I shall see that it is arranged.'

As he escorted her outside Mariella saw Xavier standing several yards away, her face beginning to burn as he looked at the prince and then allowed his glance to drift with slow and deliberate insolence over her, assessing her as though…as though she were a piece of…of flesh he was contemplating buying, Mariella recognised.

'Highness!'

'Xavier.' As the two men exchanged greetings Mariella turned to leave, but somehow Xavier had moved and was blocking her way.

'I see that you do not have Fleur with you!'

'No,' Mariella agreed coldly. 'She is in the crèche. I am just on my way to collect her.'

'You know Miss Sutton, Xavier? I hadn't realised. I am about to avail myself of her exceptional services, and she has promised me something extremely innovative.'

Mariella winced as she recognised from his expression just what interpretation Xavier had put on the prince's remarks. Excusing herself, she managed to push her way past Xavier, but to her consternation he only allowed her to take a few steps into the shadows cast by one of the pavilions before catching up with her and taking hold of her arm.

'My word, but you are a witch! The prince is renowned for his devotion to his wife and yet he speaks openly of entering a relationship with you!'

Mariella did not dignify that with an answer. Instead she bared her teeth at him in a savage little smile as she told him sweetly, 'There, you see, you need not have gone to all that trouble to protect your cousin. There is no need for you to go running to him now to tell him all about your sordid and appalling behaviour towards me. After all, once he gets to hear about the fact that the prince is paying for my...expertise...'

'You dare to boast openly about it?' Xavier was gripping her with both hands now, his fingers digging into the vulnerable flesh of her upper arms.

To her own surprise Mariella discovered that winding Xavier up was great fun and she was actually enjoying herself.

'Why shouldn't I?' she taunted him. 'I am proud of the fact that my skills are so recognised and highly thought of, and that I am able to earn a very respectable living for myself by employing them!'

As his fingers bit even harder into her arms she viewed the ominous white line around his mouth with a dangerous sense of reckless euphoria.

'In fact, in some circles I have already made quite a name for myself.'

She had gone too far, Mariella realised as her euphoria was suddenly replaced with apprehension.

'You are proud of being known as a high-class whore? Personally I would have classed you merely as an expensive one!'

Mariella was just about to slap him when he said, 'If you strike me here you could well end up in prison, whereas if I do this...'

She gasped as he bent his head and subjected her to a savagely demanding kiss, arching her whole body back as she fought not to come into contact with his, and lost that fight. In the shadows of the pavilion he used his physical strength to show her what she already knew—that despite his rage and contempt he was physically aroused by her! Just as she was by him?

He released her so abruptly that she almost stumbled. As he turned away from her he reached into his robe and removed a wallet, opening it to throw down some money.

White-faced, Mariella stared at him. Deep down inside herself she knew that she had deliberately incited and goaded him, but not for this.

'Pick it up!' he told her savagely.

Mariella took a deep breath and gathered what was left of her dignity around her. 'Very well,' she agreed calmly. 'I am sure the charity will be grateful for it,

Xavier. I understand it helps to support abandoned children.'

She prayed that he would think the glitter in her eyes was caused by her contempt and not by her tears.

Silently Xavier watched her go. His own behaviour had shocked him but he was too stubbornly proud to admit it—and even more stubbornly determined not to acknowledge what had actually caused it.

How could he admit to jealousy over the favours of such a woman? How could he acknowledge that his own desire to possess her went far, far beyond the physical desire for just her body? He could not and he did not intend to do so!

CHAPTER SEVEN

'A FRIEZE?'

The prince frowned as he looked at Mariella.

It was three days since the charity breakfast, and two since she had visited the new enclosure.

After what had happened with Xavier, the temptation to simply pack her bags and return home had been very strong, but stubbornly she had refused to give in to it.

It wasn't her fault that he had totally misinterpreted things. Well, at least not entirely! And besides... Besides, the commission the prince was offering her had far too much appeal for her as an artist to want to turn it down, never mind what her agent was likely to say!

So instead of worrying about Xavier she had spent the last two days working furiously on the idea she had had for the prince's new enclosure.

'The semi-circular walkway that leads to the enclosure would be perfect for such a project,' she told him. 'I could paint your horses there in a variety of different ways, either in their boxes, or in a string. I have spoken to your trainers and grooms and they have told me that they all have their individual personalities and little quirks, so if I painted them in a string I could include some of these. Solomon in particular, they tell me, does not like anyone else to lead the string, and then Saladin will not leave his box until his groom has removed the cat who is his stable companion. Shazare can't tolerate other horses with white socks, and—'

85

The prince laughed. 'I can see how well you have done your research, and, yes, I like what you are suggesting. It will be an extremely large project, though.'

Mariella gave a small shrug.

'It will allow me to paint the animals lifesize, certainly.'

'It will need to be done in time for the official opening of the stables.'

'And when will that be?' Mariella asked him.

'In around five months' time,' he told her.

Mariella did a quick mental calculation, and then exhaled in relief. That would give her more than enough time to get the work completed.

'It would take me about a month or two to finish. It has to be your decision, Highness,' she informed him diplomatically.

'Give me a few days to think about it. It is not that I don't like the idea. I do, but in this part of the world, we still put a great deal of store on ''face'', and therefore, no matter now innovative the idea, if it is not completed on time, then I shall lose face in the eyes of both my allies and my competitors. I certainly have no qualms about your work or your commitment to it, though.'

He needed time to check up on her and her past record of sticking to her contracted time schedules, Mariella knew, but that didn't worry her. She was always extremely efficient about sticking to a completion date once it was agreed.

The nursemaid provided by the prince to look after Fleur whilst she had been working smiled at her as she went to collect the baby.

'She is a very good baby,' the young woman told Mariella approvingly.

Once she was back in the Beach Club bungalow, Mariella tried to ring Tanya to both update her on Fleur's progress and to tell her about her work, but she was only able to reach her sister's message service.

If the prince did give her this commission, then at least she would be earning enough to ensure that Tanya did not have to work away from home. She knew her sister wanted to be independent, but there were Fleur's needs to be considered as well, and besides…

She was going to miss Fleur dreadfully when the time came to hand her back to her mother, Mariella acknowledged. She was just beginning to realise what her determination never to become involved in a permanent relationship was going to mean to her in terms of missing out on motherhood.

A little nervously, Mariella smoothed down the fabric of her skirt. She had arrived at the palace half an hour ago to see the prince, who was going to give her his verdict on whether or not he wanted her to go ahead with the frieze.

A shy nursemaid had already arrived to take Fleur from her, and now Mariella peeped anxiously at her watch. Fleur hadn't slept very well the previous night and Mariella suspected that she was cutting another new tooth.

'Miss Sutton, His Highness will see you now.'

'Ah, Mariella…'

'Highness,' Mariella responded as she was waved onto one of the silk-covered divans set around the walls of the huge audience room.

Almost immediately a servant appeared to offer her

coffee and delicious-looking almond pastries glistening with honey and stuffed with raisins.

'I am pleased to inform you that I have decided to commission you to work on the frieze,' the prince announced. 'The sooner you can complete it, the better—we have lots of other work to do before the official opening.'

Quickly Mariella put down her coffee-cup and then covered it with her hand as she saw that the hovering servant was about to refill it.

Whilst he padded away silently the prince frowned.

'However, there is one matter that is of some concern to me.'

He was still worrying about her ability to get the work finished on time, Mariella guessed, but instead of confirming her suspicions the prince got up and picked up a newspaper from the low table in front of him.

'This is our popular local newspaper,' he told her. 'Its gossip column is a great favourite and widely read.'

As he spoke he was opening the paper.

'There is here a report of our charity breakfast, and, as you will see, a rather intimate photograph of you with Sheikh Xavier Al Agir.'

Mariella's heart bumped against the bottom of her chest, her fingers trembling slightly as she studied the photograph the prince was showing her.

It took her several seconds to recognise that it had been taken when she and Xavier had been quarrelling, because it looked for all the world as though they were indeed engaged in a very intimate conversation, their heads close together, her lips parted, Xavier's head bent towards her, his gaze fixed on her mouth, whilst Fleur, whom she was holding in her arms, beamed happily at him.

Even though she had not eaten any of the pastries, Mariella was beginning to feel sick.

The article accompanying the photograph read:

Who was the young woman who Sheikh Xavier was so intimately engaged in conversation with? The sheikh is known for his strong moral beliefs and his dedication to his role as leader of the Al Agir tribe, and yet he was seen recently at the prince's charity breakfast, engaged in what appeared to be a very private conversation with one specific female guest on two separate occasions! Could it be that the sheikh has finally chosen someone to share his life? And what of the baby the unknown young woman is holding? What is her connection with the sheikh?

'In this country, unlike your own, a young woman alone with a child does cause a certain amount of speculation and disapproval. It is plain from the tone of this article that the reporter believes you and Xavier to be Fleur's parents…' the prince told Mariella, his voice very stern.

'But that is not true, Your Highness. We are not,' Mariella protested immediately. 'Fleur is my niece.'

'Of course. I fully accept what you are saying, but I think for your own sake that some kind of formal response does need to be made to this item. Which is why I have already instructed my staff to get in touch with the paper and to give them the true facts and to explain that Fleur is in fact your niece and that you are in Zuran to work for me. Hopefully that will be an end to the matter!'

*   *   *

Mariella frowned as for the third time in as many hours her sister's mobile was switched onto her message-taking service.

Why wasn't Tanya returning her calls?

Because of the length of time it was going to take her to complete the frieze, it had been decided that, instead of her returning to England as had originally been planned, she and Fleur should remain in Zuran so that she could commence work immediately.

The prince had announced that she would be provided with a small apartment and the use of a car, and Mariella was planning a shopping trip to equip both herself and Fleur for their unexpected extended stay.

Fleur's new tooth had now come through and the baby was back to her normal happy self.

Someone was knocking on the door of the bungalow and Mariella went to open it, expecting to see a member of the Beach Club's staff, but instead to her consternation it was Xavier who was standing outside.

Without waiting for her invitation he strode into the room, slamming the door closed behind him.

'Perhaps you can explain the meaning of *this* to me,' he challenged her sarcastically, throwing down the copy of the newspaper she had been reading earlier, open at the gossip column page.

'I don't have to explain anything to you, Xavier,' Mariella replied as calmly as she could.

'It says here that you are not Fleur's mother.'

'That's right,' she agreed. 'I'm not! I'm her aunt. My sister Tanya is her mother…and the woman who I have had to listen to you denouncing and abusing so slanderously and unfairly! And, for your information, Tanya is not, as you have tried to imply, some…some…

she is a professional singer and dancer, and, whilst you
may not consider her good enough for your precious
cousin, let me tell you that in my opinion he is the one
who isn't good enough for her…not for her and certainly
not for Fleur!' All the anger and anguish Mariella had
been bottling up inside her was exploding in a surge of
furious words.

'Your cousin told Tanya that he loved her and that
he was committed to her and then he left her and Fleur!
Have you any idea just what that did to Tanya? I was
there when Fleur was born, I heard Tanya cry out for
the man she loved. It's all so easy for a man, isn't it?
If he doesn't want the responsibility of a woman's love
or the child they create together, he can just walk away.
You don't know what it means to be a child growing
up knowing that your father didn't want or love you,
and knowing too that your mother could never again
be the person she was before her heart was broken. I
would never, ever let any man hurt me the way Tanya
has been hurt!'

'You wantonly and deliberately let me think that you
and Khalid were lovers,' Xavier interrupted her savagely, ignoring her emotional outburst.

'Well, at first I thought you were Fleur's father, so
I assumed you knew I wasn't Fleur's mother. But, face
it, you wanted to think the worst you could about me,
Xavier. You enjoyed thinking it! Revelled in it. I tried
to warn you that you were getting it wrong, when you
totally misinterpreted those comments by the prince!
Remember?'

'Have you any idea just what problems this is causing?' he demanded harshly.

'What I have done?' Mariella gave him a disbelieving look. 'My sister is a modern young woman who

lives a modern young woman's life. Her biggest mistake, in my opinion, was to fall in love with your wretched cousin, and yet you have talked about her as though—!' Mariella compressed her lips as she saw the flash of temper darkening his eyes.

'Are you trying to say to me that you too are a modern young woman who lives a modern young woman's life, because if you are I have to tell you—!'

Xavier broke off abruptly, remembering the character references the prince had insisted on him reading when he had stormed into the palace earlier in the afternoon, demanding an immediate audience with him.

Mariella was not only a very highly acclaimed artist, she was also, it seemed, a young woman of the highest moral integrity—in every facet of her life!

'That is none of your business,' Mariella told him angrily.

'To the contrary. It is very much my business!'

Mariella stared at him, her heart thumping.

'Fleur is my cousin's child, which makes her a member of my family. Since you are also of her blood, that also makes you a member of my family. As the head of that family I am, therefore, responsible for both of you. There is no way I can allow you to live here in Zuran alone, or work unchaperoned for the prince. Our family pride and honour would be at risk! It is my responsibility!'

'What?' Mariella looked at him in open angry contempt. 'How can you possibly lay claim to any right to pride or honour? You, a man who was quite prepared to take the mother of his cousin's child to bed, just so that you could enforce your wish to keep them apart? This has got to be some kind of joke! I mean, you…you abuse me verbally, and physically. You in-

sult and denigrate me and…and now you have the gall
to turn round and start preaching to me about pride or
honour! And as for your so-called sense of responsibility! You don't even begin to understand the meaning
of the word, as decent people understand it!'

Mariella could see the tension in his jaw, but she
suspected that it was caused by anger rather than any
sense of shame.

'The situation has now changed!'

'Changed? Because you have discovered that instead
of being, and I quote, your cousin's ''whore'' paid to
have sex with men, I am a career woman.'

'I have received a…a communication from Khalid
confirming that he is Fleur's father, and because of
that—' his mouth tightened '—I have to consider
Fleur's position, her future…her reputation!'

'Her reputation!' Mariella gave him a scathing look.
'Fleur is four months old! And anyway, His Highness
has already done everything that is necessary to stem
any potential gossip.'

'I have been to see His Highness myself to inform
him that, whilst you are here in Zuran, you will be
living beneath the protection of my roof! Naturally he
is in total agreement!'

Mariella couldn't believe her ears.

'Oh, no,' she denied, shaking her head vigorously
from side to side. 'No, no, no. No way!'

'Mariella. Please see it as a way for me to make
amends by offering you my hospitality. Besides, you
have no choice—the prince expects it.'

He meant it, Mariella recognised as she searched his
implacable features.

'I shall wait here until you have packed and then we
will return to my home. I have arranged for my wid-

owed great-aunt to act as your chaperone for the duration of your stay in Zuran.'

Her chaperone!

'I am twenty-eight years old,' she told him through gritted teeth. 'I do not need a chaperone.'

'You are a single woman living beneath the roof of a single man. There will already be those who will look askance at you having read that article.'

'At me, but not, of course, at you!'

'I am a man, so it is different,' he told her with a dismissively arrogant shrug that made her grind her teeth in female outrage.

Mariella couldn't wait to speak to her sister to tell her what had happened!

Right now, though, Mariella dared not take the risk of defying him! He could, after all, if he so wished, not merely put his threats into action, but also take Fleur from her here and now if he chose to do so!

It took her less than half an hour to pack their things, a task she performed in seething silence whilst Xavier stood in front of the door, his arms folded across his chest, watching her with smoulderingly dangerous eyes.

When she had finished she went to pick Fleur up, but Xavier got there first.

Over Fleur's downy head their gazes clashed and locked, Xavier's a seething molten grey, Mariella's a brilliantly glittering jade.

The limousine waiting for them was every bit as opulent looking as the one the prince had sent for her, although Mariella was surprised to discover that Xavier was driving it himself.

Somehow she had not associated him with a liking for such a luxurious showy vehicle. She had got the impression that his tastes were far, far more austere.

But, as she had discovered, beneath his outwardly cold self-control a molten, hot passion burned, which was all the more devastating for being so tightly chained.

It didn't take them long to reach the villa, but this time the gates were opened as they approached them and they swept in, crunching over a gravel drive flanked by double rows of palm trees.

The villa itself was elegantly proportioned, its design restrained, and Moorish in inspiration, Mariella noticed with unwilling approval as she studied its simple lines with an artist's eye.

A pair of wrought-iron gates gave way to a gravelled walled courtyard, ornamented with a large central stone fountain.

Stopping the car, Xavier got out and came to open her own door. A manservant appeared to deal with her luggage, and a shy young girl whom Xavier introduced to her as Hera, and who, he told her, would be Fleur's nanny. Smiling reassuringly at the nanny he handed Fleur to her before Mariella could stop him.

She certainly held Fleur as though she knew what she was doing, Mariella recognised, but even so! A pang of loss tightened her body as she looked at Fleur being held in another woman's arms.

'Fleur doesn't need a nanny,' she told Xavier quickly. 'I am perfectly capable of looking after her myself.'

'Maybe so, but it is customary here for those who can afford to do so to provide the less well off amongst our people with work. Hera is the eldest child in her family, and her mother has recently been widowed. Are you really willing to deprive her of the opportunity to help to support her siblings, simply because you are afraid of allowing anyone else to become emotionally close to Fleur?'

As he spoke he was ushering her into the semi-darkness of the interior of the villa. Mariella was so shocked and unprepared for his unexpectedly astute comment that she stumbled slightly as her eyes adjusted to the abrupt change from brilliant sunlight to shadowy darkness.

Instantly Xavier reached for her, his hand gripping her waist as he steadied her. Her dizziness must be something to do with that abrupt switch from lightness to dark, Mariella told herself, and so too must her accompanying weakness, turning her into a quivering mass of over-sensitive nerve endings, each one of them reacting to the fact that Xavier was touching her. Confused blurred images filled her head: Xavier, naked as he swam, Xavier leaning over her as he held her down on the bed, Xavier kissing her until she ached for him so badly her need was a physical pain.

Her need? She did not need Xavier. She would never, never need him. Never... She managed to pull herself free of him, her eyes adjusting to the light enough for her to see the cold disapproval with which he was regarding her.

'You must take more care. You are not used to our climate. By the end of this month the temperature will be reaching forty degrees Celsius, and you are very fair-skinned. You must be sure always to drink plenty of water, and that applies to Fleur as well.'

'Thank you. I do know not to allow myself to get dehydrated,' Mariella told him through gritted teeth. 'I

Live the emotion™

Anytime. Anywhere.

send for your **2 FREE ROMANCE BOOKS!**

See Details Inside...

The Romance & Presents Collection...

We'd like to introduce you to the Romance-Presents collection, a wonderful combination of Harlequin Romance® and Harlequin Presents® books.
Your 2 FREE BOOKS will include 1 book from each series in the collection:

HARLEQUIN ROMANCE®:
Tender love stories— the essence of heartwarming romance.

HARLEQUIN PRESENTS®:
These stories are intense, international and passionate.

Your 2 FREE BOOKS have a combined cover price of over $8.00 in the U.S. and over $9.00 in Canada, but they're yours FREE!

GET A *Free* MYSTERY GIFT...

We can't tell you what it is...but we're sure you'll like it! A FREE gift just for giving the Harlequin Reader Service® Program a try!

Visit us online at
www.eHarlequin.com

Your FREE Gifts include:

- 1 Harlequin Romance® book!
- 1 Harlequin Presents® book!
- An exciting mystery gift!

► DETACH AND MAIL CARD TODAY! ►

©2003 HARLEQUIN ENTERPRISES LTD.
® and ™ are trademarks owned by Harlequin Enterprises Ltd.

HARLEQUIN®
Live the emotion™

Scratch off
the silver area to see what the
Harlequin Reader Service®
Program has for you.

2 FREE BOOKS
and a FREE GIFT!

YES! I have scratched off the silver area above. Please send me the **2 FREE BOOKS** and gift for which I qualify. I understand I am under no obligation to purchase any books, as explained on the back and on the opposite page.

346 HDL DU35   126 HDL DU4M

FIRST NAME   LAST NAME

ADDRESS

APT.#   CITY

STATE/PROV.   ZIP/POSTAL CODE

(H-RP-07/03)

Offer limited to one per household. Subscribers may not receive free books from a series in which they are currently enrolled. All orders subject to approval. Books received may vary. Credit or debit balances in a customer's account(s) may be offset by any other outstanding balance owed by or to the customer.

THE HARLEQUIN READER SERVICE® PROGRAM—Here's how it works:

Accepting your 2 free books and gift places you under no obligation to buy anything. You may keep the books and gift and return the shipping statement marked "cancel." If you do not cancel, about a month later we'll send you 6 additional books from the Romance-Presents collection, which includes 3 Harlequin Romance books and 3 Harlequin Presents books, and bill you just $20.73 in the U.S., or $24.12 in Canada, plus 25¢ shipping and handling per book. That's a total saving of 15% off the cover price! You may cancel at any time, but if you choose to continue, every month we'll send you 6 more books from the Romance-Presents collection, which you may either purchase at the discount price or return to us and cancel your subscription.
*Terms and prices subject to change without notice. Sales tax applicable in N.Y. Canadian residents will be charged applicable provincial taxes and GST.

DETACH AND MAIL CARD TODAY!

If offer card is missing write to: Harlequin Reader Service, 3010 Walden Ave., P.O. Box 1867, Buffalo NY 14240-1867

BUSINESS REPLY MAIL
FIRST-CLASS MAIL   PERMIT NO. 717-003   BUFFALO, NY

POSTAGE WILL BE PAID BY ADDRESSEE

HARLEQUIN READER SERVICE
3010 WALDEN AVE
PO BOX 1867
BUFFALO NY 14240-9952

NO POSTAGE
NECESSARY
IF MAILED
IN THE
UNITED STATES

am a woman, not a child, and as such I am perfectly capable of looking after myself. After all, I've been doing it for long enough.'

The look he gave her made her feel as though someone had taken hold of her heart and flipped it over inside her chest.

'Yes. It must have been hard for you to lose your mother and your stepfather having already lost your father at such a young age...'

'Lost my father?' Mariella gave him a bitter look. 'I didn't "lose" him. He abandoned my mother because he didn't want the responsibilities of fatherhood. He was never any true father to me, but he broke my mother's heart—'

'My own parents died when I was in my early teens—a tragic accident—but I was lucky enough to have my grandmother to help me through it. However, as we both know, the realisation that one is without parents does tend to breed a certain...independence of spirit, a certain protective defensiveness.' He was frowning, Mariella recognised, picking his words with care as though there was something he was trying to tell her. He broke off as Hera came into the reception hall carrying Fleur.

'If you will go with Hera, she will show you to your quarters. My aunt should arrive shortly.'

He had turned on his heel and was striding away from her, his back ramrod straight in the cool whiteness of his robe, leaving her no alternative other than to follow the timidly smiling young maid.

The villa obviously stretched back from its frontage to a depth she had not suspected, Mariella acknowledged ten minutes later, when she had followed the maid through several enormous reception rooms and up a flight of stairs, and then along a cloistered walk-way through which a deliciously cool breeze had flowed and from which she had been able to look down into a totally enclosed private courtyard, complete with a swimming pool.

'This is the courtyard of Sheikh Xavier,' Hera had whispered to her, shyly averting her gaze from it and looking nervous when Mariella had paused to study it.

'Normally it is forbidden for us to be here, as the women of the household have their own private entrance to their quarters...'

'Let me take Fleur,' Mariella told her, firmly taking her niece back into her own arms and relishing the deliciously warm weight of her.

A door at the end of the corridor led to another cloistered walkway, this time with views over an immaculate rose garden.

'This was the special garden of the sheikh's grandparents. His grandmother was French and the roses were from France. She supervised their planting herself.'

For Mariella the rigid beds and the formality of the garden immediately summoned up a vivid impression of a woman who was very proud and correct, a true martinet. Her grandson obviously took after her!

The women's quarters, when they finally got to them, proved to be far more appealing than Mariella had expected. Here again a cloistered walkway opened onto a private garden, but here the garden was softer, filled with sweet-smelling flowers and decorated with a pretty turreted summer house as well as the customary water features.

They comprised several lavishly furnished bedrooms, each with its own equally luxurious bathroom

and dressing room, a dining room, and a salon—
Mariella could think of no other word to describe the
delicate and ornate antique French furniture and decor
of the two rooms, which she suspected must have been
designed and equipped for Xavier's French grandmother.

On the bookshelves flanking the fireplace she could
see leather-bound books bearing the names of some of
France's most famous writers.

'The sheikh has said that you will wish to have the
little one in a room next to your own,' Hera was telling
her softly. 'He has made arrangements for everything
that she will need to be delivered. I am not sure which
room you will wish to use…'

Ignoring the temptation to tell her that she wished to
use none of them, and that in fact what she wished to
do was to leave the villa with Fleur right now—after
all, none of this was Hera's fault and it would be unfair
of her to take out her own resentment on the maid—
Mariella gave in to her gentle hint and quickly in-
spected each of the four bedrooms.

One of them, furnished in the same Louis Fifteenth
antiques as the salon, had quite obviously been
Xavier's grandmother's and she rejected it immediately. Of the three others, she automatically picked the
plainest with its cool-toned walls and simple furniture.
It had its own private access to the gardens with a small
clear pool only a few feet away and a seat next to it
from which to watch the soothing movement of the
water.

'This room?'

When Mariella nodded, Hera smiled.

'The sheikh will be pleased. This was his mother's
room.'

Xavier's mother's room! It was too late for her to change her mind, Mariella recognised.

'What…what nationality was she?' she asked Hera, immediately wishing she had not done so.

'She was a member of the tribe… The sheikh's father met her when he was travelling with them and fell in love with her…'

Fleur was beginning to make hungry noises, reminding Mariella that it was her niece she should be thinking about and not Xavier's family background.

CHAPTER EIGHT

MARIELLA stared worriedly at her mobile phone. She had just tried for the fourth time since her arrival at the villa to make contact with Tanya, but her sister's mobile was still switched onto messaging mode. She had left a message saying that she was staying at Xavier's villa, and had asked Tanya to contact her at the villa or call her cell phone. Mariella realised to her consternation that it was days since she had actually spoken to Tanya. A little tingle of alarm began to feather down her spine. What if something had happened to her sister? What if she wasn't well or had hurt herself. Or...

Quickly Mariella made up her mind. It took her quite some time to get the telephone number for the entertainments director of her sister's cruise liner, but eventually she managed to get through.

'I'm sorry, who is this speaking, please?' The firm male voice on the other end of the line checked her when Mariella had asked for Tanya, explaining that she had been unable to make contact with her via her mobile.

'I am Tanya's sister,' Mariella explained.

'I see... Well, I have to inform you that Tanya has actually left the ship.'

'Left the ship!' Mariella repeated in disbelief. 'But...where? Why...?'

'I'm sorry. I can't give you any more details. All I can say is that Tanya left of her own accord and without giving us any prior warning.'

101

From the tone of his voice Mariella could tell that he wasn't very pleased with her sister!

Thanking him for his help, she ended the call, turning to look at Fleur, who was fast asleep in her brand-new bed.

As Hera had already warned her, Xavier had instructed a local baby equipment store to provide a full nursery's worth of brand new things, all of which Mariella had immediately realised were far, far more expensive and exclusive than anything she or Tanya could have afforded.

Tanya! Where was her sister? Why had she left the ship? And why, oh, why wasn't she returning her calls?

It was imperative that she knew what was happening, and, for all her faults, her impulsiveness and hedonism, Tanya genuinely loved Fleur. It was unthinkable to Mariella that she should not make contact with her to check up on her baby.

In Tanya's shoes there was no way she would not have been on the phone every hour of every day… No way she could ever have brought herself to be parted from her baby in the first place, Mariella recognised, but then poor Tanya had had no alternative! Tanya had been determined to pay her own way.

Emotionally, she stood over Fleur looking down at her whilst she slept. Increasingly she ached inside to have a child of her own. When she had made her original vow never to put herself in a position where she could be emotionally hurt by a man, she had not foreseen this kind of complication!

Xavier frowned as he paced the floor of his study. A flood of faxes cluttered his desk, all of them giving him the same information—namely that his cousin had not been seen in any of his usual favourite haunts! Where on earth was Khalid?

Xavier was becoming increasingly suspicious that his cousin had been deliberately vague about Fleur's true paternity. Out of a desire to protect Fleur and her mother, or out of a desire to escape his responsibilities?

Surely Khalid knew him well enough to know that, even if he couldn't approve of or accept Fleur's mother, he would certainly have insisted that proper financial arrangements were made for her and Fleur, and if necessary by Xavier himself? Of course he did, which was no doubt why he had now written to Xavier informing him that he was Fleur's father.

It irked him that he had been so dramatically wrong-footed in assuming that Mariella was Fleur's mother. The security information the prince had revealed to him had made it brutally clear just how wrong he had been about her.

Here was a young woman who had shouldered the responsibility, not just of supporting herself, but of supporting her younger half-sister as well. Not a single shred of information to indicate that Mariella had led anything other than the most morally laudable life could be found! There were no unsavoury corpses mouldering away in the dusty corners of Mariella's life; in fact, the truth was that there were not even any dusty corners! Everyone who had had dealings with her spoke of her in the most glowing and complimentary terms.

And yet somehow he, a man who prided himself on his astuteness and his ability to read a person's true personality, had not been able to see any of this! True, she had deliberately deceived him, but...

But he had behaved towards her in a way that, had

he heard about it coming from another man, he would have had no hesitation in immediately denouncing and condemning him!

There were no excuses he could accept from himself! Not even the increasingly insubstantial one of wanting to protect Khalid.

Wasn't it after all true that the last thing, the last person who had been in his thoughts when he had taken Mariella to bed had been his cousin? Wasn't it also true that he had been driven, possessed...consumed by his own personal physical desire?

He could find no logical excuse or explanation for what he had done. Other than to tell himself that he had been driven by desert madness, and he felt riddled with guilt, especially for the way he had coerced her into staying with him at his villa. He would of course have to apologise formally to Mariella!

A woman who already had proved how strong her sense of duty and responsibility was. A woman with whom a man could know that the children he gave her would be loved and treasured...

He had sworn not to marry, rather than risk the hazards of a marriage that might go wrong, he reminded himself austerely.

Surely, though, it was better to offer Mariella the protection of his name in marriage rather than risk any potential damage to her reputation through gossip?

He had already provided her with sufficient protection in the form of his great-aunt as a chaperone, he reminded himself grimly. If he continued to think as he was doing right now, he might begin to suspect that he actually wanted to marry her! That he actually wanted to take her back into his bed and complete what they had already begun.

Angrily he swung round as the sudden chatter of the fax machine broke into his far too sensually charged thoughts.

'So, here we are, then. Xavier has summoned me to be your chaperone, and I am to accompany you to the palace whilst you paint pictures for His Highness, *non?*'

'Well, not exactly,' Mariella responded wryly. It was impossible for her not to like the vivacious elderly Frenchwoman who was Xavier's great-aunt and who had arrived half an hour earlier, complete with an enormous pile of luggage and her own formidable looking maid.

'I am not actually working at the palace, but at the new enclosure at the racecourse, and, to be honest, I don't agree with Xavier—'

'Agree? But I am afraid that here in Zuran we have to comply with the laws of the land, *chérie,* both actual and moral.' Rolling her eyes dramatically, she continued, 'I know how difficult I found it when I first came to live here. My sister was already married to Xavier's grandfather for several years by then. She was older than me by well over a decade. Since the death of my husband, I live both in Paris and here in Zuran. The child I understand is Khalid's?' she commented, with a disconcerting change of subject. 'He is a charming young man, but unfortunately very weak! He is fortunate that Xavier is so indulgent towards him, but you probably know Xavier does not intend to marry and he intended for Khalid's son to ultimately take over his responsibilities! It is such foolishness...'

'Xavier does not intend to marry?' Mariella questioned her.

'So he claims. The death of his own parents affected him very seriously. He was at a most impressionable age when they perished and of course my sister, his grandmother, was very much a matriarch of the old school. She was determined that he would be brought up to know his responsibilities towards his people and to fulfil them. Now Xavier believes that their needs are more important than his own and that he cannot therefore risk marrying a woman who would not understand and accept his duty and the importance of his role. Such nonsense, but then that is men for you! They like to believe that we are the weaker sex, but we of course know that it is we who are the strong ones!'

'You have great strength, I can see that! You will miss the child when you eventually have to hand her back to her mother,' she added shrewdly.

The speed of her conversation, along with the speed of her perceptiveness, was leaving Mariella feeling slightly dizzy.

'I see that you have chosen not to occupy my late sister's room. Extremely wise of you if I may say so…I could never understand why she insisted on attempting to recreate our parents' Avenue Foche apartment here! But then that was Sophia for you! As an eldest child she was extremely strong-willed, whilst I…' she paused to dimple a rueful smile at Mariella '…am the youngest, and, according to her at least, was extremely spoiled!

'You would not have liked her,' she pronounced, shocking Mariella a little with her outspokenness. 'She would have taken one look at you and immediately started to make plans to make you Xavier's wife. You do not believe me? I assure you that it is true. She

would have seen immediately how perfect you would
be for him!'

Her, perfect for Xavier? Fiercely squashing the
treacherous little sensation tingling through her,
Mariella told her quickly, 'I have no intention of ever
getting married.'

'You see? Already it is clear just how much you and
Xavier have in common! However, I am not my sister.
I do not interfere in other people's lives or try to arrange them for them! *Non!* But tell me why is it that
you have made up your mind not to marry? In Xavier's
case it is plain that it is because of the fear instilled in
him by my sister that he will not find a woman to love
who will share his dedication to his commitment to
preserve the traditional way of life of the tribe. Such
nonsense! But Sophia herself is very much to blame.
When he was a young and impressionable young man
she sent Xavier to France in the hope that he would
find a bride amongst the daughters of our own circle.
But these girls cannot breathe any air other than that
of Paris. The very thought of them doing as Xavier has
done every year of his life and travelling through the
desert with those members of the tribe who had chosen
to adhere to the old way of life would be intolerable
to them!

'Xavier needs a wife who will embrace and love the
ways of his people with the same passion with which
he does himself. A woman who will embrace and love
him with even more passion, for, as I am sure you will
already know, Xavier is an extremely passionate man.'

Mariella gave her a wary look. What was his great-
aunt trying to imply? However, when she looked at her
face her expression was rosily innocent and open.

Madame Flavel's comments were, though, arousing both her interest and her curiosity.

Hesitantly she told her, 'You have mentioned the tribe and Xavier's commitment to it, but I do not really know just what...'

'*Non?* It is quite simple really. The tribe into which Xavier's ancestor originally married is unique in its way of life, and it was the life's work of Xavier's grandfather, and would have been of his father had he not died, to preserve the tribe's traditional nomadic existence, but at the same time encourage those members of it who wished to do so to integrate into modern society. To that end, every child born into the tribe has the right to receive a proper education and to follow the career path of their choice, but at the same time each and every member of the tribe must spend some small part of every year travelling the traditional nomadic routes in the traditional way. Some members of the tribe elect to live permanently in such a fashion, and they are highly revered by every other member of the tribe, even those who, as many have, have reached the very peak of their chosen career elsewhere in the world. Within the tribe recognition and admiration are won, not through material or professional attainment, but through preservation of the old ways and traditions.

'Xavier's role as head of the tribe means, though, that he has a dual role to fulfil. He must ensure that he has the business expertise to see that the money left by his grandfather generates sufficient future income to provide financially for the tribe, and yet at the same time he must be able to hold the respect of the tribe by leading it in its ancient traditional ways. Xavier has known all his life that he must fulfil both those roles and he does so willingly, I know, but nevertheless it will be a very lonely path he has chosen to follow unless he does find a woman who can understand and share his life with him.'

Mariella had fallen silent as she listened. There was a poignancy about what she was hearing that was touching very deep emotional chords within. The Xavier his great-aunt was describing to her was a man of deep and profound feelings and beliefs, a man who, in other circumstances, she herself could respect and admire.

'*Madame,* I assure you there is really no need for you to remain here with me,' Mariella told her chaperone firmly as she studied the long corridor that was to be her canvas.

Fleur was lying in her pram playing with her toes and Mariella had pinned up in front of her, on the easel she had brought with her, the photographs she had taken of the prince's horses.

'It is for this purpose that Xavier has summoned me to his home,' Madame Flavel reminded her.

'You will be bored sitting here watching me work,' Mariella protested.

'I am never bored. I have my tapestry and my newspaper, and in due course Ali will return to drive us back to the villa for a small repast and an afternoon nap.'

There was no way she intended to indulge in afternoon naps, Mariella decided silently as she picked up her charcoals and started to work.

In her mind she already had a picture of how she wanted the frieze to look, and within minutes she was totally engrossed in what she was doing.

The background for the horses, she had now decided,

would not be the racecourse itself, but something that she hoped would prove far more compelling to those who viewed it. The background of a rolling ocean of waves from which the horses were emerging would surely prove irresistible to a people to whom water was so very, very important. Mariella hoped so. His Highness had certainly liked the idea.

It wasn't until her fingers began to ache a little with cramp that she realised how long she had been working. Madame Flavel had fallen asleep in the comfortable chair with its special footstool that Ali had brought for her, her gentle snores keeping Fleur entranced.

Smiling at her niece, Mariella opened the bottle of water she had brought with her and took a drink. Where was Tanya? Why hadn't she got in touch with her?

The door to the corridor opened to admit Hera and Ali.

'Goodness, is it lunchtime already?' Madame Flavel demanded, immediately waking up.

Reluctantly Mariella started to pack up her things. She would much rather have continued with her work than return to the villa, but she was very conscious of Madame Flavel's age and the unfairness of expecting her to remain with her for hours on end.

CHAPTER NINE

BY THE end of the week Mariella was beginning to find her enforced breaks from her work increasingly frustrating.

'It disturbs me that you are so determined not to marry, *chérie*,' Madame Flavel was saying to her as she worked. 'It is perhaps because of an unhappy love affair?'

'You could say that,' Mariella agreed wryly.

'He broke your heart, but you are young, and broken hearts mend...'

'It wasn't my heart he broke, but my mother's,' Mariella corrected her, 'and it never really mended, not even when she met and married my stepfather. You see, she thought when my father told her that he loved her he meant it, but he didn't! She trusted him, depended on him, but he repaid that trust by abandoning us both.'

'Ah, I see. And because of the great hurt your father caused you, you are determined never to trust any man yourself?' Madame Flavel commented shrewdly. 'Not all men are like your father, *chérie*.'

'Maybe not, but it is not a risk I am prepared to take! I never want to be as...as vulnerable as my mother was...never.'

'You say that, but I think you fear that you already are.'

Mariella was glad of Ali's arrival to put an end to what was becoming a very uncomfortable conversation.

* * *

It was two o'clock in the afternoon and Madame Flavel was taking her afternoon nap.

Mariella walked restlessly round the garden. She was itching to get on with the frieze. She paused, frowning slightly. And then, making up her mind, hurried back inside, pausing only to pick up Fleur.

Ali made no comment when she summoned him to tell him that she intended to go back to the enclosure, politely opening the door of the car for her. Stepping outside was like standing in the blast of a hot hair-dryer at full heat.

The car was coolly air-conditioned, but outside the heat shimmered in the air, the light bouncing glaringly off the buildings that lined the road.

Like the car, the enclosure was air-conditioned, and as soon as Ali had escorted her inside and gone Mariella began to work.

A moveable scaffolding had been erected to allow her to work on the upper part of the wall, and she paused every now and again to look down from it to check on Fleur, who was fast asleep. Her throat felt dry and her hand ached, but she refused to allow herself to stop. In her mind's eye she could see the finished animal, nostrils flaring, his mane ruffled by the wind, the sea foaming behind him as he emerged from the curling breakers.

Somewhere on the edge of her awareness she was vaguely conscious of a door opening, and quiet but ominously determined footsteps. Fleur made a small sound, a gurgle of pleasure rather than complaint, which she also registered, her hand moving quickly as she fought to capture the image inside her head. This horse, the proudest and fiercest of them all, would not tolerate any competition from the sea. He would challenge its power, rearing up so that the powerful muscles of his quarters and belly were visible... Fleur was chattering happily to herself in baby talk, and Mariella was beginning to feel almost light-headed with concentration. And then just as she was finishing something a movement, an instinct made her turn her head.

To her shock she saw that Xavier was standing beside Fleur watching her.

'Xavier...'

She took a step forward and then stopped, suddenly realising that she was still on the scaffolding.

'What...what are you doing here?' she demanded belligerently to cover her own intimate and unwanted reaction to him.

'Have you any idea just how much you distressed Cecille by ignoring my instructions?' he demanded tersely.

Mariella looked away from him. She genuinely liked his great-aunt, and hated the thought that she might have upset her.

'I'm sorry if she was upset,' she told him woodenly, her own feelings breaking through her tight control as she gave a small despairing shake of her head.

'I promised His Highness that the frieze would be completed as soon as possible; your aunt is elderly. She likes to spend the afternoon resting, when I need to be here working! Whether you believe this or not, Xavier, I too have a...a reputation to protect.'

'In that case why didn't you simply come to me and explain all of this to me instead of behaving like a child and waiting until my aunt's back was turned?'

Mariella frowned. What he was saying sounded so...so reasonable and sensible she imagined that anyone listening to him would have asked her the same question!

'Your behaviour towards me has hardly encouraged me to…to anticipate your help or co-operation,' she reminded him as she went to climb down from the scaffolding, surreptitiously trying to stretch her aching muscles.

'Although she herself refuses to acknowledge it, my aunt is an elderly lady,' Xavier was continuing, breaking off suddenly to mutter something beneath his breath she couldn't quite catch as he strode forward.

'Be careful,' he warned her sharply. 'You might…'

To her own chagrin, as though his warning had provoked it, the scaffolding suddenly wobbled and she began to slip.

As she gave a small instinctive gasp of shock Xavier grabbed hold of her, supporting her so that she could slide safely to the floor.

Mariella knew that the small near-accident was her own fault and that she had worked for too long in one position, without stopping to exercise her cramped muscles, and her face began to burn as she anticipated Xavier's triumphant justification of his insistence that she was chaperoned, but instead of saying anything he simply continued to hold her, one hand grasping her waist, the other supporting the small of her back, where his fingers spread a dangerously intoxicating heat right through her clothes and into her skin.

Dizzily Mariella closed her eyes, trying to blot out the effect the proximity of him was having on her, but, to her consternation, instead of protecting her all it did was increase her vulnerability as sharply focused mental images of him taunted and tormented her, their ef-

fect on her so intense that she started to shake in reaction to them.

'Mariella? What is it? What's wrong?' she heard
Xavier demanding urgently. 'If you feel unwell…'

Immediately Mariella opened her eyes.

'No. I'm fine,' she began and then stopped, unable
to drag her gaze away from his mouth, where it had
focused itself with hungry, yearning intensity.

She knew from his sudden fixed silence that Xavier
was aware of what she was doing, but the shrill alarm
bells within her own defences, which should have
shaken her into action, were silenced into the merest
whisper by the inner roar of her own aching longing.
No power on earth, let alone that of her own will, could
stem what was happening to her and what she was
feeling, Mariella recognised distantly, as her senses
registered the way Xavier's grip on her body subtly
altered from one of non-sexually protective to one of
powerfully sensual. She could feel the hot burn of his
gaze as it dropped to her own mouth, and a sharp series
of little shivers broke through her. Without even thinking about it she was touching her lips with the tip of
her tongue, as though driven by some deep pre-
programmed instinct to moisten them. She was trembling, her whole body galvanised by tiny sensual ripples of reaction and awareness that made her sway
slightly towards him.

She saw a muscle twitch in his jaw and raised her
hand to touch it with her fingertips, her eyes wide and
helplessly enslaved.

'Mariella!'

She felt him shudder as he drew breath into his
lungs, her body instinctively leaning into his as weakness washed over her.

His mouth touched hers, but not in the way she had remembered it doing before.

She had never known there could be so much sweet tenderness in a kiss, so much slow, explorative warmth, so much carefully suppressed passion just waiting to burn away all her resistance. She wanted to lose herself completely in it…in him.

She gave a small cry of protest as Xavier's ears, keener than hers, picked up the sound of someone entering the gallery, and he pushed her away.

Caught up in the shock of what she had experienced, Mariella watched motionless as Xavier went over to where Ali, his chauffeur, was hovering.

Lifting her hand, she touched her own lips, as though unable to believe what had happened…what she had wanted to happen. She had wanted Xavier to kiss her, still wanted him to kiss her, her body aching for him in a hundred intimate ways that held her in silent shock. She and Xavier were enemies, weren't they?

He was walking back to her and somehow she had to compose herself, to conceal from him what was happening to her.

She felt as though she were drowning in her own panic.

'We must get back to the villa, immediately,' he told her curtly.

Instantly her panic was replaced by anxiety.

'What is it?' she demanded. 'Has something happened to your aunt?'

She started to gather up her things, but he stopped her, instructing her tersely, 'Leave all that.'

He was already picking up Fleur, his body language so evident of a crisis that Mariella forbore to argue. Her stomach was churning sickly. What if something had happened to his great-aunt, perhaps brought on by her own stubborn determination to ignore his dictates? She would never forgive herself!

Falling into step beside him, Mariella almost had to run to keep up with him.

They drove back to the villa in silence, Mariella's anxiety increasing to such a pitch that by the time they finally turned into the courtyard of the villa she felt physically sick.

Giving some sharp order to Ali, in Arabic, Xavier got out of the car, turning to her and telling her equally shortly, 'Come with me.'

Even Fleur seemed to have picked up on his seriousness, and fell silent in his arms, her eyes huge and dark.

Please let Cecille be all right, Mariella prayed silently as the huge double doors to the villa were thrown open with unfamiliar formality and she followed Xavier into its sandalwood-scented coolness.

Without pausing to see if she was following him, Xavier headed for the anteroom that opened out into what Mariella now knew was the formal salon in which he conducted his business meetings.

Unusually two liveried servants were standing to either side of the entrance, their expressionless faces adding both to Mariella's anxiety and the look of stern formality she could see on Xavier's face, giving it and him an air of autocratic arrogance so reminiscent of the first time she had seen him that she automatically shivered a little.

Expecting him to stride into the room ahead of her, Mariella almost bumped into him when he suddenly turned towards her. A little uncertainly she looked at him, unable to conceal her confusion when he reached out his hand to her and beckoned her to his side.

Holding Fleur tightly, she hesitated for a second before going to join him. Wide as the entrance to the salon was, it still apparently necessitated Xavier standing so close to her that she could feel the heat of his body against her own as he gave the servants an abrupt nod.

The doors swung open, the magnificence of the room that lay beyond them dazzling Mariella for a moment, even though she had already peeped into it at Madame Flavel's insistence.

It was everything she had ever imagined such a room should be, its walls hung with richly woven silks, the cool marble floor ornamented with priceless antique rugs. The light from the huge chandeliers, which Madame Flavel had told Mariella had been made to Xavier's grandmother's personal design, dazzled the eyes as it reflected on the room's rich jewel colours and ornate gilding. Luxurious and rich, the decor of the salon had about it an unmistakable air of French elegance.

It was a room designed to awe and impress all those who entered it and to make them aware of the power of the man who owned it.

As her eyes adjusted to the brilliance Mariella realised that two people were standing in front of the room's huge marble fireplace, watching Xavier with obvious apprehension as they clung together.

Disbelievingly Mariella stared at them.

'Tanya,' she whispered, her voice raw with shock as she recognised her sister.

Her sister looked tanned and expensive, Mariella noticed, the skirt and top she was wearing showing off her body. She was wearing her hair in a new, fashionably tousled style, and it glinted with a mix of toning blonde highlights.

She was immaculately made up, her fingernails and toenails shining with polish, but it was the man standing at Tanya's side on whom Mariella focused most of her attention. He was shorter than Xavier and more heavily built, she guessed immediately that he must be Khalid, Xavier's cousin and Fleur's father.

'Khalid,' Xavier acknowledged curtly, with a brief nod in the other man's direction, confirming Mariella's guesswork. 'And this, I assume, must be…'

'My wife,' Khalid interrupted him, holding tightly to Tanya's hand as he continued, 'Tanya and I were married three days ago.'

'Honestly, Mariella, I just couldn't believe it when we docked at Kingston and Khalid came on board. At first I totally refused to have anything to do with him, but he kept on persisting and eventually…'

It was less than twenty-four hours since Mariella had learned that her sister and Khalid were now married, and Tanya was updating her on what had happened as they sat together in the garden of the villa's women's quarters, whilst Fleur gurgled happily in her carrier.

'Why didn't you tell me what was going on when I telephoned you?' Mariella asked her.

Tanya looked self-conscious.

'Well, at first I wasn't sure just what was going to happen—I mean…Khalid was there and he was being very sweet, admitting that he loved me and that he regretted what he had done, but…'

'And then you left that message on my cell phone saying you were here with Xavier, and I was worried that you might say something to him and that he would find a way of parting me and Khalid again…'

'Have you any idea how worried about you I've been?' Mariella asked her.

Tanya flushed uncomfortably.

'Well, I had hoped that you'd just think I wasn't returning your calls because I was so busy… It didn't occur to me that you'd ring the entertainments director…'

'Tanya, you didn't ring me to check on Fleur for days. Of course I was worried…'

'Oh, well, I knew she'd be fine with you, and I did listen to your messages. But Khalid… Well, we needed some time to ourselves, and Khalid insisted… Please don't be cross with me, Ella. You've never been in love so you can't understand. When Khalid left me I thought my life was over. I'm not like you. I need to love and be loved. I don't think I'll ever forgive Xavier for what he did.'

'Xavier didn't physically compel Khalid to abandon you and Fleur, Tanya,' Mariella heard herself pointing out to her sister almost sharply.

The look Tanya gave her confirmed her own realisation of what she had done.

'How can you support him, Ella?' Tanya demanded. 'He threatened to stop Khalid's allowance; he would have left me and Fleur to starve,' she added dramatically.

'That's not true, Tanya, and not fair either,' Mariella felt bound to correct her, but she couldn't quite bring herself to tell her sister that it was her own opinion that Khalid was both weak and self-indulgent and that he had selfishly put his own needs before those of his lover and their child. She could see already the begin-

nings of a sulky pout turning down the corners of
Tanya's mouth and her heart sank. She had no wish to
quarrel with her sister, but at the same time she
couldn't help feeling that Tanya wasn't treating her
own behaviour with regard to her maternal responsibilities towards Fleur anywhere near as seriously as she
should have been doing.

'Well, we're married now and there's nothing that
Xavier can do about it! And he knows it!'

Mariella knew that this was not true and that Xavier
could have carried out his threat to stop paying Khalid
his allowance, and also remove him from his sinecure
of a job. However, she also knew from what Madame
Flavel had innocently told her that Xavier had not done
so because of Fleur.

'Oh, and you'll never guess what,' Tanya told her
excitedly. 'I haven't had the opportunity to tell you yet,
but Khalid is insisting on taking me for an extended
honeymoon trip. We're going to take Fleur with us, of
course, and then once we get back I suppose we will
have to make our home here in Zuran, but Khalid has
promised me that we'll get away as often as we can.
He says that we can have our own villa and that I can
choose everything myself! Oh, and look at my engage-
ment ring. Isn't it beautiful?'

'Very,' Mariella agreed cordially as she studied the
huge solitaire flashing on her sister's hand.

'I can't tell you how happy I am, Ella,' Tanya
breathed ecstatically. 'And you have looked after my
darling baby so well for me. I have missed you so
much, my sweet,' Tanya cooed, blowing kisses to her
daughter. 'Your daddy and I can't wait to have you all
to ourselves.'

As she listened to her sister a small shadow crossed

Mariella's face, but she was determined not to spoil Tanya's happiness by letting her see how much she was dreading losing Fleur.

'It all sounds very exciting,' she responded, forcing a smile as she looked up and saw the expectant look on her sister's face.

'When will you be leaving?'

'Tomorrow! Everything's already arranged. Khalid just wanted to come to Zuran to tell Xavier about our marriage, and to collect Fleur, of course...'

'Of course,' Mariella agreed hollowly.

'Ella, I can't thank you enough for looking after Fleur for me. We're both really grateful to you, aren't we, Khalid?'

'Yes, we are,' her new brother-in-law agreed.

Mariella was still holding Fleur, not wanting to physically part with her until she absolutely had to, whilst Tanya said her goodbyes to Madame Flavel and Xavier.

Tanya was still behaving very coolly towards Xavier, only speaking to him when she had to do so.

'Darling, can you take Fleur out to the car?' she instructed Khalid.

Mariella could feel herself stiffening as Khalid went to take the baby from her, and, whether because of that or because as yet Fleur was not used to her father, as he reached for her the little baby suddenly screwed up her face and started to cry.

Immediately Khalid pulled back from her looking flustered and irritable.

'Here, let me take her!'

Xavier quietly removed Fleur from Mariella's arms, before she could object. He smiled down at Fleur and soothed her, whilst she gazed back at him wide-eyed, her tears immediately ceasing.

Out of the corner of her eye Mariella saw that Tanya had started to glower at Xavier, obviously resenting the fact that Fleur was more comfortable with him than with her father, but before she could say anything Khalid was urging her to hurry.

They went out to the car together, Xavier still holding Fleur, Mariella wincing in the blast of hot air.

As soon as she got into the car, Tanya held out her arms to him for Fleur, but to Mariella's surprise, instead of handing Fleur to Tanya, Xavier gave her to Mariella.

Mariella could feel her eyes burning with emotional tears, her throat closing up as her feelings threatened to overwhelm her. It was almost as though Xavier could sense how she felt and wanted to give her one last precious chance to hold Fleur before she had to part with her.

Bending her head, she kissed her niece and then quickly handed her over to her sister.

When the car taking them to the airport finally pulled away, Mariella could only see it through a blur.

'Let's get out of this wind,' she heard Xavier telling her when the car had finally disappeared from sight.

If he was aware of her tears he was discreet enough not to show it, simply ushering her back to the villa without making any other comment.

However, once they were inside, Mariella took a deep breath and made her voice sound as businesslike as she could as she told him, 'I'll make arrangements to leave just as soon as I can arrange somewhere else to stay.'

'What on earth are you talking about?' Xavier de-

manded sharply. 'Nothing has changed. You are still a
single young woman who is a member of my family,
and as such your place is still here beneath my roof
and my protection! This should be your home whilst
you're in Zuran,' Xavier told her.

Mariella opened her mouth to argue with him and
then closed it again. It was just because she was feeling
so upset about losing Fleur that his statement was giving her this odd sense of heady relief, she told herself
defensively. It had nothing to do with…any other reason. Nothing at all!

Mariella was dreaming. She was dreaming that she was
all alone in an unfamiliar room, lying on a large bed
and crying for Fleur, and then suddenly the door
opened and Xavier came in. Walking over to the bed,
he sat down beside her and reached out for her hand.

'You are crying for the child,' he told her softly. 'But
you must not. I shall give you a child of your own to
love. Our child!' As she looked at him he started to
touch her, smoothing the covers from her naked body
with hands that seemed to know just how to please her.
Bending his head, he started to kiss her, a slow, mag-
ically tender kiss, which quickly began to burn with
the heat of a fierce passion. She could feel her whole
body trembling with need and longing! And not just
for the child he had promised her, but for Xavier himself!

His hands cupped her breasts, his grey eyes liquid
with arousal as he gazed at them, shockingly sensual
words of praise falling from his lips as he whispered
to her how much he wanted her. He kissed each rosy
crest, savouring their shape and sensitivity with his lips

and tongue until she was clinging to him, digging her
nails into his back as she submitted to her own desire.

Possessively she measured the strong length of his
arms with her fingertips, expelling her breath on a
shuddering sigh as his tongue rimmed her belly and his
hand covered her sex, waiting, aching, wanting.
Beneath her hand she could feel him harden as she
touched him, torn between wanting to explore him and
wanting to feel him deep inside her as he ignited the
spark of life that would be their child. But as she
reached for him, suddenly he pulled away, abandoning
her. Desperately she cried out to him not to leave her,
her body chilled and shaking, tears clogging her throat
and spilling from her eyes. Abruptly Mariella woke up.

Somehow in her sleep she had pushed away the bedclothes, which was why she was now shivering in the
coolness of the air-conditioning. The tears drying stick-
ily on her face and tightening her skin were surely
caused by the fact that she was missing Fleur and not
because she had been dreaming about Xavier...about
loving him and losing him! She would never allow herself to be that much of a fool! But physically she was
affected by him, she could not deny that! Fiercely she
tried to tense her body against its own betraying ache
of longing. Xavier was a man who, even she had to
acknowledge, took his responsibilities and his commit-
ments very seriously. A man whose passions...

Stop it, she warned herself frantically. What was she
doing thinking like this? Feeling like this?

Wide awake now, she got out of bed, and was halfway toward Fleur's now empty cot before she realised
what she was doing. It was only right that Fleur should

be with her parents, but she ached so to be holding her small body. She ached so for a child of her own, she admitted.

Tiredly Mariella flexed the tense, aching muscles in her neck and shoulders as she sat beside the small pool in the women's courtyard. She had worked relentlessly on the frieze over the last two weeks, driven by a compulsion she hadn't been able to ignore, and now knew that she would be able to finish the project well ahead of time.

The prince had arrived to inspect her progress just before she had left and she had seen immediately from his expression just how impressed he was by what she was doing.

'It is magnificent…awe-inspiring,' he had told her enthusiastically. 'A truly heart-gripping vision.'

'I'm glad you like it,' Mariella had responded prosaically, but inwardly she had been elated.

Elated and too exhausted to eat her dinner, she reminded herself ruefully as she reached up to try and massage some relief into her aching neck, tensing as she saw Xavier walking towards her.

'I have just come from seeing His Highness,' he told her. 'He wanted to show me your work. He is most impressed, and rightly so. It is magnificent!'

His uncharacteristic praise stunned Mariella, who stared at him, her turquoise eyes shadowed and wary.

'Has your sister been in touch with you yet to reassure you that Fleur is well?' Xavier continued.

Not trusting herself to speak, Mariella shook her head and then winced as her tense, locked muscles resisted the movement.

Quick to notice her small betraying wince, Xavier

demanded immediately, 'You're in pain. What is it? What's wrong?'

'My muscles are stiff, that's all,' Mariella replied.

'Stiff. Where? Let me see?'

Before she could object he was sitting down next to her, his fingers moving searchingly over her shoulders, expertly finding her locked muscles.

'Keep still,' he said when she instinctively tried to pull away. 'I am not surprised you are in so much pain. You work too hard! Drive yourself too hard. Worry too much about others and allow them to abuse your sense of responsibility towards them!'

Swiftly Mariella turned her head to look at him.

'You are a fine one to accuse me of that!' she couldn't help pointing out.

For a moment they looked at one another in mutual silence. She was learning so much about this man, discovering so many things about him that changed her whole perception of what and who he was.

He couldn't have been more wrong about Mariella, or misjudged her more unfairly, Xavier acknowledged as he looked down into her eyes. Her sister, in contrast, was exactly what he had expected her to be, and typical of his cousin's taste in women. The more cynical side of his nature felt that, not only were they suited to one another, but that they also deserved one another in their mutual selfishness and lack of any true emotional depth.

Mariella, on the other hand... He had never met a woman who took her responsibilities more seriously, or who was more fiercely protective of those she loved. When she committed herself to a man she would commit herself to him heart and soul. When she loved a man, she would love him with depth and passion and her love would be for ever...

'Your sister should have been in touch with you. She must know how much you are missing Fleur,' he told Mariella abruptly.

Mariella tensed, immediately flying to Tanya's defence as she told him fiercely, 'She is Fleur's mother. She doesn't have to consult me about...anything. This holiday will give the three of them an opportunity to bond together as a family. Tanya and Khalid are Fleur's parents and...'

'I miss Fleur too,' Xavier stopped her gruffly, his admission astonishing her. 'And in my opinion she would be much better off here in a secure environment with those who know her best, rather than being dragged to some fashionable resort where she will probably be left in the care of hotel staff whilst her parents spend their time enjoying themselves!'

'You are being unfair,' Mariella protested, and then winced as Xavier started to knead the knots out of her muscles, making it impossible for her to move.

'No. I am being honest,' he corrected her. 'And when Khalid returns you may be sure that I shall be making it very plain to him that Fleur needs a secure family environment!'

Xavier would make a wonderful father, Mariella conceded, and then stiffened as she tried to reject the messages that knowledge was giving her! After all, like her, Xavier had no intentions of ever getting married!

'Your muscles are very badly knotted,' she heard him telling her brusquely as his thumbs started to probe their way over the tight lumps of pain.

It was heaven having the tension massaged from her body, Mariella acknowledged, and no doubt what he

was doing would be even more effective if she wasn't
trying to tense herself against those dangerous sensa-
tions that had nothing whatsoever to do with any kind
of work-induced muscle ache, and everything to do
with Xavier himself.

The longer he touched her, the harder she was finding it to control her sexual reaction to him.

His thumbs stroked along her spine, causing her to
shudder openly in response. Immediately his hands
stilled.

'Mariella.'

His voice sounded rough and raw, the sensation of
his breath against her skin bringing her out in a rash
of sensual goose-bumps. Was she only imagining that
she could hear a note of hungry male desire in his
voice?

She couldn't trust herself to speak to him, just as she
didn't dare to turn round, but suddenly he was turning
her, holding her, finding her mouth with his own and
kissing her with a silent ferocity that made her tremble
from head to toe as her body dissolved in a wash of
liquid pleasure that ran through her veins, melting any
resistance.

The hands that had so clinically massaged her shoulders were now caressing her flesh beneath her loose
top in a way that was anything but clinical! A savage,
relentless ache began to torment her body. The warm,
perfumed night air of the garden was suddenly replaced
by the aroused male scent of Xavier's body and
Mariella reacted to it blindly, wrenching her mouth
from beneath his and burying her face in the open
throat of his robe so that she could breathe it—him—
in more deeply, her lips questing for the satin warmth

of his skin, her moan of pleasure locked in her throat as she gave her senses their head.

Beneath her lips his flesh felt firm and hot, the muscles of his throat taut, the curve where it met his shoulder tempting her to bite delicately into it. She heard him groan as his hand covered her breast, her nipple swelling eagerly against his palm. She felt the warmth of the night air against her skin as he pushed her simple cotton robe out of the way, her whole body shuddering in agonised pleasure as he cupped her breast and lowered his mouth to her waiting nipple.

The pleasure that surged through her tightened her body into a helpless yearning arc of longing, exposing her slender feminine flesh to his gaze and touch, offering her up to them, Mariella recognised distantly as she shook with hunger for him. Wanting him like this seemed so natural, and right, so inevitable, as though it were something that had been destined to happen.

Lifting her hand, she touched his face, their gazes meeting and locking, silently absorbing one another's need. The look in his eyes made her body leap in eager heat, the sensation of the slightly rough rasp of his jaw against her palm as he turned his face to kiss it filling her with a thousand erotic images of how it was going to feel, to have him caressing even more sensitive and intimate parts of her body. She was, she realised, trembling violently, as Xavier stroked his hands down her back and lifted her against his body so that she could feel its hard arousal. She ached so badly for the feel of him inside her, for the fulfilment of his possession of her, the completion. His mouth was on her breast, her nipple, caressing it in a way that made her cry out for the hot, deep suckle of a more savage pleasure.

In the moonlight Xavier could see the swollen softness of her mouth and her breast, his breath catching in his lungs as his gaze travelled lower, to where the delicate mound of her sex seemed to push temptingly against the fine cotton of her briefs.

The thought of sliding his hand beneath them and holding her, parting the delicately shaped lips and opening up her moist inner self to his touch, his kiss, sent a shudder of hot need clawing through him. In the privacy of this garden he could show her, share with her, give her the pleasure he could see and feel her body was aching for. But here in his garden, in his villa, where she was under his protection, a member of his family…a woman as off limits as any of the carefully guarded daughters of his friends.

His hand was already splaying across her sex, his thumb probing tantalizingly.

Hot shafts of molten quivers darted from the point where Xavier's hand rested so intimately on her to every sensitive nerve ending in her body. Within herself Mariella could feel her own femaleness expanding rhythmically in longing. More than anything else she wanted him there inside her. More than anything else she wanted him…

Her raw sound of shocked protest broke the silence as Xavier suddenly released her.

'I already owe you one apology for my…my inappropriate behaviour towards you,' she heard him telling her curtly. 'Now it seems that I am guilty of repeating that behaviour. It will not…must not happen again!'

As he stood up and turned away from her, Mariella wondered if he was trying to reassure her—or warn her! Her face and then her whole body burned hot with mortified misery.

Her throat was too choked with emotion for her to

be able to say anything, but in any case Xavier was already leaving, walking across the garden to the small, almost hidden doorway that led through into his own quarters, and to which only he had the key.

Was she too destined to be a secret garden to which only he held the key?

Fiercely she resisted the dangerous and unwanted thought. It was simply sex that had driven her…a physical need…a perfectly normal response to her own sexuality. There was nothing emotional about what she had felt. Nothing.

Pacing the floor of his own room, Xavier came to an abrupt decision. Since he couldn't trust himself to be in the same place as Mariella and not want her, then he needed to put a safe distance between them, and the best way for him to do that would be for him to return to his desert oasis.

CHAPTER TEN

'IT IS almost a week since he left and still Xavier remains at the oasis.'

Mariella forced herself to concentrate on her work instead of reacting to Madame Flavel's comments.

The prince had come to see how she was progressing earlier in the week and he had brought his wife and their young family with him. The sight of the four dark-haired and dark-eyed children clustering round their parents had filled her with such a physical ache of longing that she had felt as though her womb had actually physically contracted.

She was desperate to have her own child, Mariella recognised. And not just because she was missing Fleur. Fleur's birth might have detonated her biological clock, setting it ticking away with such frantic urgency, but the longing she felt now was beginning to consume her, eating into her dreams and her emotions.

Now she felt she understood why she had wanted Xavier so much. Her body had recognised him as a perfect potential baby provider! Knowing that had in a way eased a lot of the anxiety she had been feeling; the fear she couldn't bear to admit that she might actually have fallen in love with him. Now, though, she felt secure that her emotional defences had not been breached. Now it was easy for her to admit to herself just how much she had wanted him and how much she still wanted him. She wanted him because she wanted him to give her a child!

It made so much sense! Didn't she remember reading somewhere that a woman naturally and instinctively responded to the ancient way in which nature had programmed her and that was to seek the best genes she could for her child? Quite obviously her body had recognised that Xavier's genes were superlative and her brain fully endorsed her body's recognition.

And this of course was why she was being bombarded by her body and her brain with messages, longings, desires, images that all pointed in the same direction. Xavier's direction! Her maternal urges were quite definitely on red alert!

'Xavier has telephoned to say that he will be remaining at the oasis for another week,' Xavier's great-aunt informed Mariella with a small sigh as they sat down for dinner. 'It must be dull here for you, *chérie* with only your work to occupy you and me for company.'

'Not at all,' Mariella denied.

'*Non?* But you do miss *la petite bébé?*'

Now it was Mariella's turn to sigh.

'Yes, I do,' she admitted.

'Then perhaps you should consider having *enfants* of your own,' Madame Flavel told her. 'I certainly regret the fact that I was not blessed with children. I envied my sister very much in that respect. I have to confess I cannot understand why two people like Xavier and yourself, who anyone can see are born to be parents, should decide so determinedly against marriage.

'You are working very hard on your frieze. It would do you good to have a few days off.'

She *had* been working very hard—but if truth were

told, the frieze was practically finished. But Mariella had been painstakingly refining it to make sure it was absolutely perfect. Could she take a few days off? To do what? Have even more time to miss Fleur and to ache for a child of her own? Even more time to wish passionately that Xavier had not brought an end to their intimacy before they had... If only she had pressed him a little harder, persuaded...seduced him to the point where he had not been able to stop, she considered daringly, then right now she could already be carrying within her the beginnings of her own child!

Restlessly her thoughts started to circle inside her head. Once they had finished eating Madame Flavel retired to her own room, leaving Mariella to walk through their private garden on her own. If only Xavier were here in the villa now, she could go to him. And what? Demand that he take her to bed and impregnate her?

Oh, yes, she could just see him agreeing to that!

Why would she have to demand? She was a woman, wasn't she? And Xavier was a man... He had already shown her that he could be aroused to desire for her...

But he wasn't here, was he? He was at the oasis.

The oasis... Closing her eyes, Mariella allowed herself to picture him there. That night when he had thought that she was Tanya, he had come so close to possessing her. Her whole body was aching for him now, aching with all the ferocity of a child-hungry woman whose womb was empty!

Irritably, Mariella threw down her sketch-pad, chewing on her bottom lip as she glowered at the images she had drawn: babies...all of them possessing Xavier's unmistakable features. She had hardly slept all night, and when she had it had merely been to be tormented by such sensually erotic dreams of Xavier that they had made her cry out in longing for him. It was as though even her dreams, her own subconscious, were reinforcing her desire for Xavier's child.

In fact the only thing about her that was still trying to fight against that wanting was…was what? Fear… Timidity… Did she really want to look back in years to come and face the fact that she had simply not had the courage to reach out for what she wanted?

After all, it wasn't as though she would be doing anything illegal! She had no intention of ever making any kind of claim on Xavier—far from it! She actively wanted to be left to bring up her child completely on her own. All she wanted from him was a simple physical act. All she had to do…

All she had to do was to make it impossible for him to resist her! And whilst he was at the oasis he would be completely at her sensual mercy! It was even the right time of the month—she was fertile.

A wildly bold plan was beginning to take shape inside her head, and the first step towards it meant an immediate shopping trip, for certain…necessities! There was a specific shop she remembered from a previous trip to the busy souk in the centre of the city, which specialised in what she wanted!

Slightly pink-cheeked, Mariella studied the fine silk kaftan she was being shown by the salesgirl, so fine that it was completely sheer. Surely the only thing that stopped it from floating away was the weight of the intricate and delicate silver beading and embroidery around the neck and hem and decorating the edges of the long sleeves.

It was a soft shade of turquoise, and designed to be
worn—the salesgirl had helpfully explained without so
much as batting an elegantly kohled eyelid—over a
matching pair of harem trousers. Their cuffs and waist-
band had been embroidered to match the kaftan itself.
It was quite plainly an outfit designed only to be worn
in private and for the delectation of one man. The
sheerness of the fabric would leave one's breasts totally
revealed—and Mariella had not missed the strategically
embroidered rosettes, which she doubted would do
anything more than merely make a teasing pretence of
covering the wearer's nipples—and as for the fact that
the harem pants incorporated an embroidered and
beaded v-shaped section at the front, which she had an
unnerving suspicion would draw attention to rather
than protect, any wearer's sex…

'And then, of course, there is this,' the salesgirl told
her, showing Mariella a jewelled piece of fabric, which
she helpfully explained was self-adhesive so that the
wearer could easily fix it to her navel.

Mariella gulped. Her normal sleeping attire when she
wore any tended to be sturdily sensible cotton pyjamas.

'Er… No…I don't think…it's quite me,' she heard
herself croaking, her courage deserting her. Seducing
Xavier was going to be hard enough without giving
herself the kind of self-conscious hang-up wearing that
kind of outfit would undoubtedly give her!

'I…I was thinking of something more…more
European,' she explained ruefully to the salesgirl.

'Ah, yes, of course. There is a shop in the shopping
centre run by my cousin which specialises in French
underwear. I shall tell you how to find it.'

Mariella sensed that the girl was amused by her self-
consciousness, but there was no way she intended to

pay a sheikh's ransom for an outfit that would take more courage to wear than going completely naked!

The souk was busy, and she paused on her way back through it to admire the wares on some of the other stalls, especially the rugs.

There was far more to seduction than merely wearing a harem outfit, she tried to comfort herself as she headed for the modern shopping centre. Far, far more. Sight was just one of man's senses, after all.

By the time she finally returned to the villa Mariella felt totally exhausted. She was now the proud owner of a perfume blended especially for her, and a body lotion guaranteed to turn her skin into the softest silk; she had also given in to the temptation to buy herself some new underwear, from the harem outfit seller's cousin, in the shopping mall. French and delicately feminine without making her feel in any way uncomfortable. Low-cut French knickers might not be as openly provocative as beaded harem trousers but they did have the advantage of being perfect to wear underneath her jeans!

It didn't take her very long to pack. All she said to Hera when she summoned her was that she wanted her to hand the note she was giving her to Madame Flavel when she woke up from her afternoon nap.

By that time she should have safely reached the oasis, and her note was simply to calm the older lady's fears and told her only that Mariella had driven out to the oasis because there was something she wanted to discuss with Xavier.

She took a taxi to the four-wheel drive rental office, where the car she had organised earlier by telephone was waiting for her.

This time she made sure she had the radio tuned in to the local weather station, but thankfully no sandstorms were forecast.

Taking a deep breath, she started the car's engine.

With a small oath, Xavier pushed the laptop away and stood up. He had come to the oasis to put a safe distance between himself and Mariella but all his absence from her was doing was making him think about her all the more.

Think about her! He wasn't just thinking about her, was he?

The tribe were currently camped less than thirty miles away and on a sudden impulse he decided to drive over and see them. The solitude of his own company was not proving to be its usual solace. Everywhere he looked around the oasis he could see Mariella. There might be a cultural gap between them, but, like him, she had a very strong sense of responsibility, and like him she would not give either her heart or herself easily. Like him, too, once she was committed, that commitment would be for ever. And did she also ache for what they had so nearly had and lie away at night wanting…needing, afraid to admit that those feelings went way, way beyond the merely physical? And if she did, then… Could she love him enough to accept his duty to the tribe, and with it his commitment to his role in life…to accept it and to share it? Dared he lay before her the intensity of his feelings for her? His love? Could he live with himself if his secret fears proved to be correct and his love for her overwhelmed his sense of duty?

Switching off the laptop, he reached for his Jeep keys.

* * *

She couldn't ever remember a time when she had felt more nervous, Mariella acknowledged as she urged the four-wheel drive along the familiar boulder-strewn track. Up ahead of her she could see the pavilion and her heart lurched, slamming into her ribs. What if Xavier simply refused to be seduced and rejected her? What if…?

For a moment she was tempted to turn the four-wheel drive round and scuttle back to the city. Quickly she reminded herself of sexual tension stretching between them in the garden of the villa. He had wanted her then, and had admitted as much to her!

She had half expected to see him emerging from the pavilion as he heard her drive up, but there was no sign of him.

Well, at least he wouldn't be able to demand that she turn round and drive straight back, she comforted herself as she parked her vehicle and climbed out, going to the back to remove her things, and then standing nervously staring at the pavilion.

Perhaps if she had timed things so that she had arrived in the dark… Some seductress she was turning out to be, she derided herself as she took a deep breath and walked determinedly towards the chosen fate.

Five minutes later she was standing facing the oasis, unwilling to accept what was patently obvious. Xavier was not here! No Xavier, no four-wheel drive, no seduction, no baby!

A crushing sense of disappointment engulfed her. Where was he? Could he have changed his mind and returned to the city despite informing his great-aunt that he intended to stay on at the oasis? How ironic it would be if by rushing out here so impulsively she had actually denied herself the opportunity of achieving what she wanted!

But then she remembered that his laptop was still inside the pavilion, and surely he would not have left that behind if he had been returning home? So where was he?

The sun was already a dying red ball lying on the horizon. Soon it would be dark. There was no way she was going to risk driving all the way back without the benefit of daylight!

So what exactly was she going to do? Spend yet another evening enduring her rebellious body's clamouring urgency for the fulfilment of its driving need? It had simply never occurred to her that he wouldn't be here!

The pavilion was so intimately a part of him. Dreamily, she trailed her fingertips along the chair he used when working at the laptop. The air actually seemed to hold an echo of his scent, a haunting resonance of his voice, and she felt that, if she closed her eyes and concentrated hard enough, she could almost imagine that he was there... She could certainly picture him behind her tightly closed eyelids. But it wasn't his mental image she wanted so desperately, was it?

She knew she ought to eat, but she simply wasn't hungry. She was thirsty, though.

She went into the kitchen and opened a bottle of water. Fine grains of sand clung to her skin, making it feel gritty. Hardly appropriate for a would-be siren! The long drive in the brilliant glare of the desert sun had left her eyes feeling tired and heavy. Like her body, which felt tired and heavy and empty. A sense of dejection and failure percolated through her.

Slowly, she walked out of the kitchen intending to

return to the living area, but instead found herself being drawn to the 'bedroom.' Standing in the entrance, she looked achingly around it.

A fierce shudder that became an even fiercer primal ache gripped her as she looked at the bed and remembered what had happened there. It was just her biology that was making her feel like this, her fiercely strong maternal desire. That was all, and of course it was only natural that that urge should manifest itself in this hungry desire for the man whose genes it had decided it wanted, she reassured herself as she was confronted with the intensity of her longing for Xavier.

Just thinking about him made her go weak, made her want him there so that she could bury her lips in the warm male flesh of his throat and slide her hands over the hard, strong muscles of his arms and his back, and then down through the soft dark hair that covered his chest and arrowed over his belly to where…

She needed a shower, Mariella decided shakily. A very cool shower!

'Safe travelling, Ashar.' Xavier smiled ruefully as he embraced the senior tribesman whilst the others went about the business of breaking camp ready to begin the long slow journey across the desert.

'You could always come with us,' Ashar responded.

'Not this time.' Xavier shook his head.

All around him he could hear the familiar sounds of the camp, the faint music of the camel bells, the orderly preparations for departure. The tribe would travel through the night hours whilst it was cool, resting the herd during the heat of the day.

Ashar's shrewd brown eyes surveyed him.

Ashar remembered Xavier's grandfather as well as

his father. Alongside his respect for Xavier as his leader ran a very deep vein of paternal affection for him.

'Something troubles you—a woman, perhaps? The tribe would rejoice to see you take a wife to give you sons to follow in your footsteps as you have followed in those of your grandfather and your father.'

'If only matters were that simple, Ashar.' Xavier grimaced.

'Why should they not be? This woman, you are afraid perhaps that she will not respect our traditions, that she will seek to divide your loyalties? If that is so then she is not the one for you. But knowing you as I do, Xavier, I cannot believe that there could be a place in your heart for a woman such as that. You must learn to trust what is in here,' he told him, touching his own heart with his hand. 'Instead of believing only what is in here.' As he touched his hand to his head Xavier hid a wry smile. Ashar had no idea just how dangerously out of control his emotions were becoming!

He waited to see the tribe safely on their way before climbing in his vehicle to drive back to the oasis.

A sharply crescented sickle moon shared the night sky with the brilliance of the stars. Diamonds studded onto indigo velvet. For Xavier it was during the night hours that the desert was at its most awesome, and mystical, a time when he always felt most in touch with his heritage. His ancestors had travelled these sands for many, many generations before him, and it was his duty, his responsibility to ensure that they did so for many, many generations to come. And that was not something he could achieve from behind the walls of a high-rise air-conditioned office, and certainly not from the fleshpots of the world as Khalid would no doubt choose to do. No, he could only maintain and honour the tribe's traditional way of life by being a part of it, by sharing in it, and that was something he was totally committed to doing. He must not deviate from that purpose. But his feelings, his love for Mariella could not be denied, or ignored. The strength of them had initially shocked him, but he had now gone from shock to the grim recognition that it was beyond his power to change or control the way he felt.

He saw Mariella's vehicle as he drove up to the oasis. Parking next to it, he got out and studied it warily. He did not encourage anyone to visit him when he was at the oasis and he was certainly not in the mood for uninvited guests, right now! Where and who was its driver?

Frowning, he headed for the pavilion, not needing to waste any time lighting the lamps to illuminate the darkness, his familiarity with it enough to take him from the entrance to the opening to the bedroom without breaking his stride.

Mariella was lying fast asleep in the middle of the bed, where she had curled up in exhaustion like a small child. The white robe she was wearing was Xavier's and it drowned her slender body. She had lit one of the lamps, which illuminated her face, showing her bone structure and the thick darkness of her silky eyelashes. In the enclosed heat, Xavier could smell the scent of her, and of his own instant reciprocal desire for her.

Xavier's hand tightened convulsively on the cord that fastened the curtain to the bedroom's entrance, whilst his heart tolled in slow, heavy beats. If he had any sense he would pick her up and carry her straight out to the Jeep and then drive back to the city with her without stopping!

He let the heavy curtain drop behind him, enclosing them both in the sensual semi-darkness.

Standing next to the bed, he looked down at Mariella.

Something, some instinct and awareness, disturbed Mariella's sleep, making her frown and stir, her eyes opening.

'Xavier!'

Relief…and longing flooded through her. Automatically she struggled to sit up, her arms and legs becoming tangled in the thick folds of Xavier's robe as she did so.

'What are you doing here?' Xavier demanded harshly.

'Waiting for you,' Mariella told him. 'Waiting to tell you how much I want you, and how much I hope you want me.'

She watched as his eyes turned from steel to mercury and recognised that she had caught him off guard.

'You drove all the way out here to tell me that!'

His voice might be curt and unresponsive, but Mariella could see the way his jaw tightened as he turned his head away from her, as well as feel his betraying tension. Tiny body-language signs, that was all she knew, but instinctively she knew she had an advantage to pursue!

'Not to tell you, Xavier,' she corrected him boldly. 'To show you…like this…'

Standing up, she went to him, letting the robe slide from her body as she did so. She had never envisaged that she would ever feel such a pride in her nakedness, her femaleness, such a sense of power and certainty, an awareness of how much a man's still silence could betray how very, very tightly leashed he was keeping his desire.

She was standing in front of him and he hadn't moved. For a moment she almost lost her courage but then she saw it, the way he clenched his hand and tried to conceal his involuntary reaction.

Quickly she raised herself up on her tiptoes and cupped his face with her hands. Never in a thousand lifetimes could she have behaved like this simply for her own gratification, for the indulgence of her own sexual or emotional feelings, but she was not doing it for them, for herself, she was doing it for the child she so desperately wanted to give life! Silently she looked up into his eyes, her own openly reflecting her desire. Very deliberately she let her gaze drop to his mouth. There was no need for her to manufacture the sharp little quiver of physical reaction that pierced her, tightening her belly.

She brushed her lips against his—slowly, savouring the delicate sensual contact between them, refusing to be put off by his lack of response, drawing from her inner self to focus totally on the pleasure it was giving her to explore the shape and texture of his mouth. Very quickly her senses took over, so that it was desire that led her to stroking his bottom lip with her tongue tip rather than calculation, the same desire that drove her to trace tiny kisses along the shape of his mouth and then draw her tongue lightly along that shape.

Xavier couldn't endure what she was doing to him! Mentally he willed her to stop, but instead she opened her mouth over his and started to kiss him properly! Lost in what she was doing, what she was enjoying,

Mariella took her time, putting her whole self into showing him just how hungry for him she was.

And then sickeningly, she could feel the rejecting hostility of his body, and for a heart-rocking second when he raised his hands she thought he was going to push her away. She suspected that he had thought so too, because suddenly in his eyes she saw both his shock and his raw, burning hunger.

He could never be a man who would be a passive lover, Mariella recognised on a deep shudder of pleasure as his hands imprisoned her and his mouth fought hers for control.

How little he realised that her surrender was really her victory, she rejoiced as his tongue thrust urgently between the lips she had parted for him.

'I can't believe that you've done this,' she heard him saying thickly.

'I had to,' Mariella whispered back. After all, it was the truth. 'I had to be with you, Xavier…like this…as a woman.'

He had released her to look at her, and now he lifted his hand to her face. Instantly Mariella caught hold of his wrist and turned her head to run her tongue tip over his fingertips.

She saw the way his skin stretched over his cheekbones, running hot with colour, his chest lifting and falling as savagely as though he had been deprived of oxygen. His forefinger rubbed over her bottom lip, and when she sucked on it his whole body jerked fiercely.

'I want to see you, Xavier,' she told him softly. 'I want to touch you…taste you…I want. I want you to take me to bed and pleasure me, fill me.'

Taking his hand, she placed it against her naked breast.

'Please,' she whispered. 'Please now, Xavier. Please…'

'This is crazy. You know that, don't you?' she heard him mutter. 'You are not your sister, you do not… I have not… I am not prepared…' His voice had become thick and raw as he bent his head to kiss the exposed curve of her shoulder, her throat, his hands sliding down her back to pull her urgently against him.

'There is nothing for you to worry about,' she told him.

She felt light-headed with the intensity of her own longing—but she only felt like that because she wanted his child, she was quick to reassure herself. That, after all, was what was driving her, motivating her, even if that motivation was manifesting itself in an increasingly urgent need to touch him and be touched by him, to allow herself to luxuriate in the slow and delicious exploration of every bit of his skin, absorbing its heat, its feel, the essence of him through the sensitivity of her own pores. So that her child, their child could be impregnated through her with those memories of his father he would never otherwise be able to have?

Ruthlessly she stifled that thought. Her child would not need a father to be there. He or she only needed a father to provide that life.

What he was doing was reckless to the point of insanity, Xavier knew that, but he also knew that he couldn't resist her, that he had ached for her, yearned for her too long to deny himself the soft, sweet, wanton feel of her in his arms…his bed…

But once he had held her, loved her, he also knew that he would never be able to let her go. Could she accept his way of life…adapt to it? Would she?

She was kissing him with increasing passion, stringing tiny, delicately tormenting little kisses around his throat, her tongue tip carefully exploring the shape of his Adam's apple, her fingers kneading the flesh of his upper arm with unconscious sensuality. Xavier recognised his senses on overload from her deliberately erotic seduction.

Mariella gave a small startled gasp as Xavier suddenly lifted her bodily in his arms, so that her mouth was on a level with his own as he took it in a hotly demanding and intimate kiss.

Helplessly she succumbed to it, feeling the desire he was arousing inside her run through her veins as sweetly as melting honey. He lifted her higher, kissing her throat, his lips moving lower to the valley between her breasts, before trailing with heart-hammering slowness and delicacy to first one eagerly waiting, quivering crest and then the other, and then back again, this time to lap tormentingly at her nipple with his damp tongue tip; the leisurely languorous journey repeated again and again until her whole body was crying out in agonised frustration.

Unable to stand the sensual torment any more, when his lips teased delicately at her nipple she buried her hands in the thick darkness of his hair and held his mouth against her body.

Surely he must feel the fierce rhythms pulsing through her flesh; surely he must know how much she wanted him?

Her hands tugged at his clothes, her voice whispering a soft torrent of aroused female longing that swamped Xavier's defences.

His hands helped hers to quickly remove the layers of clothing that separated them.

When she finally saw the naked gleam of his flesh

in the lamp-lit room, Mariella sucked in her breath on a small sob of shocked pleasure.

In wonder she studied him as tiny but openly visible quivers betrayed her body's excited reaction to him. So compulsively absorbed in gazing at him, she was oblivious to the effect her sensual concentration was having on Xavier himself.

'If you are deliberately trying to torment me and test my self-control by looking at me like that, then I warn you that both it and I have just about reached my limit,' he told her thickly.

'Now! Are you going to come to me and put into action all those dangerously seductive promises your eyes are giving me, or do I have to come to you and make you make good those promises, because, I warn you, if I do have to then I shall be demanding payment with full interest penalties,' he added huskily.

For a moment Mariella couldn't do anything. Xavier was watching her as she had been watching him. Excitement exploded inside her. She took a step towards him and then another, measuring his reaction as best she could, but it wasn't easy given the extent of her own intense arousal.

She was only a breath away from him now, close enough to reach out her finger and draw the tip of it recklessly down his body, teasing the silky body hair.

'You don't know how much I've wanted to do this,' she breathed truthfully.

'No? Well, I certainly know how much I've wanted you to do it,' Xavier responded throatily, 'and how much I've wanted to…'

He gasped and shuddered as her fingertip stroked lower, and suddenly in the space of one single heartbeat she was lying on the bed, with Xavier arching over her.

'Play with fire like that and you'll make us both burn,' he told her, his eyes darkening as he groaned. 'Do you know what seeing that look in your eyes does to me? Do you know how much I've wanted to see just what colour they turn when I touch you like this?'

Mariella hadn't realised just how ready she was for his intimate caress until she felt his hand stroke softly over her quivering belly, his fingers gently touching the swollen mound of her sex, his gaze pinioning hers as he parted the lips of her sex and began to caress her.

Mariella knew that she cried out, she knew too that her body arched to his touch actively seeking it, eagerly opening to it, but it was only a vague, distant knowledge, at the back of her awareness. Her self was concentrated on the mind-exploding battle to accept the intensity of her own feelings.

Frantically she reached for Xavier. Touching him, holding him, wrapping herself around him as she pressed passionate kisses against his skin, willing, aching for him to complete what he had begun.

And when he did enter her, moving into her, filling her moist sheathed muscles, filling her with such a soaring degree of pleasure that they and she clung to him, wanting to wring every infinitesimal sensation of pleasure from him, it was like nothing she had ever imagined feeling, a pleasure beyond any known pleasure, a sensation beyond any experienced sensation, a driven need that shocked her in its wanton compulsion as she urged him to drive deeper, harder, breaching every last barrier of her body until she knew instinctively that he could not and would not withdraw from her without giving her body the satisfaction it now craved.

They moved together, his thrusts carrying them both, delivering a pleasure so intense she could scarcely bear it, crying out against it at the same time as she abandoned herself to it.

She heard his guttural cry of warning and felt her body open up completely to him, the first tiny shudders of her orgasm sensitising her to the pulse of his, to the knowledge that she was receiving from him what she had so much wanted.

Was it that knowledge that made her orgasm so intense, so fierce that she felt almost as though she could not endure so much pleasure?

Long after it should have been over, the aftermath continued to send little shudders of sensation through her, shaking her whole body as she lay locked in Xavier's arms.

She had done it, instinctively she knew it. Her child, of the desert and of a man who was equally compelling, equally dangerous, had been given life.

Reluctantly, Mariella opened her eyes. She could hear a shower running, and her whole body ached with an unfamiliar heaviness.

'So you are awake!'

She stiffened as she saw Xavier coming towards her, his hair damp from his shower, a towel wrapped carelessly round his hips.

Leaning towards her, he bent his head to kiss her. He smelled of soap and clean, fresh skin and her body quivered helplessly in reaction to him.

'Mmm...'

He kissed her again, more lingeringly, his hand stroking down over her bare arm.

The quivers became open shudders of erotic pleasure as he pulled the bedclothes back.

She had got what she wanted, and so surely she shouldn't be feeling like this now that there wasn't any need for her to want him!

The towel was sliding from his hips, quite plainly revealing the fact that he most definitely wanted her.

A sharp and unmistakable thrill of female excitement gripped her muscles.

It was just nature's way of making doubly sure, Mariella told herself hazily as his hand cupped her breast, his thumb and forefinger teasing the already eagerly taut crest of her nipple. That was all, and, since nature wanted to be doubly sure, then obviously she must give in to her urgings. Urgings that were demanding that she experience the pleasure Xavier had given her the night before, and right now...

His hands were on her hips, holding her, lifting her. Already Mariella was anticipating the feel of him inside her, longing for it and for him. Needing him.

'There will be things we shall need to discuss once we return to the city.'

'Mmm...' Mariella agreed, too satiated to lift her head off the pillow as Xavier turned to brush a kiss across her mouth.

She looked so tempting lying there in his bed, her face soft with satisfaction and her eyes heavy with their lovemaking, he acknowledged, ruefully aware of the way in which his senses were still reacting to her.

It would be all too easy to let the desire between

them flare into life again, but there were practicalities that had to be considered.

'Mariella.' The abrupt note in his voice caught her attention. 'Because of my position as leader of our tribe, I have always believed that I do not have the…freedoms of other men. I could never commit myself to a relationship with a woman who might not be able to understand or accept my duties and responsibilities to my people. Nor could I change my way of life, or…'

'Xavier, there's no need for you to say any more,' Mariella checked him swiftly. Her heart was pounding heavily, a sharp, bitter little pain, piercing her even though she was fighting against admitting to it, stubbornly refusing to listen to the message it was trying to give her.

'I would never ask you or any other man to do any such thing! And I can assure you that you need have no fear that I might misconstrue what's happened. I shan't. I am most definitely not looking for any kind of commitment from you.'

Only the commitment of conceiving his child, she admitted inwardly.

'In fact, commitment is the last thing I want.' Assuming a casualness that defied everything she had always inwardly believed in, she gave a small shrug and told him, 'We are both adults. We wanted to have sex. To satisfy a…a physical need… And…now that we have done so, I don't think there is any purpose in us holding a post-mortem, and even less in getting involved in needless discussions about the wherefores of why neither of us want a committed relationship. Truthfully, Xavier, I don't want to marry you any more than you want to marry me! In fact, I shall never marry.' Mariella delivered the words in a strong voice underpinned with determination.

'What?'

Why was Xavier looking at her like that? Where was the relief she had expected—the cool acceptance of her claim that they had come together merely to slake their sexual appetite for one another? Xavier was looking at her with a mingling of barely controlled fury and bitterness.

'What are you saying?' she heard him demanding savagely. 'You are not your sister, Mariella! You are not one of those shallow, surface-living women who think only of themselves; who give in to their need to experience what they want when they want, who go from man to man, bed to bed without...whose whole way of life—' He paused and shook his head.

'You are not like her! You don't even know what you are talking about! Mere physical sex is not something...'

Mariella could see and feel the intensity of his growing anger, and she could also feel her own increasingly disturbing reaction of panic and pain to it, but she refused to allow herself to be intimidated by them.

'I am not going to argue with you, Xavier. I know how I feel, and what I do and don't want from life.'

Well, that was the truth, wasn't it? She did know what she wanted, and she had every hope that last night had given her...

'Do you really expect me to believe that you drove all the way out here just because you wanted sex?'

'Why not?' Mariella shrugged. 'After all, I could hardly have come to your room at the villa, could I?' she pointed out, trying to make herself react as though she were the woman she was trying to be—a woman who thought nothing of indulging her sexual appetite as and when she wanted to do so!

'This was the perfect opportunity!'

Xavier was looking at her as though he would dearly love to make her take back her words, Mariella recognised uneasily. It had to be his male pride that was making him react in such an unexpected manner, she decided. Men were quite happy to use women for sexual pleasure without being emotionally committed to them, but apparently they didn't like it very much when they thought that they were the ones being used.

Her legs began to tremble shakily as she mentally digested his reaction and tried to imagine what he might say—and do if he knew that she hadn't even actually wanted him out of sexual lust, and that the desire that had really driven her had been her own female need to conceive his child!

Somehow instinctively she knew that the reaction she was seeing now would be nothing when compared with what he was likely to do were he ever to discover the truth!

The unexpected shrill sound of his mobile ringing broke into the thick silence stretching tensely between them.

Out of good manners Mariella turned away whilst he answered the call, but she could tell from the sound of his curt replies that it involved some kind of crisis.

Her instincts were confirmed when he ended the call and told her abruptly, 'There is a problem with the tribe—a quarrel between two of the younger men, which needs to be dealt with. I shall have to drive out to do so immediately.'

'That's okay. I can find my own way back to the city,' Mariella assured him.

'This matter isn't closed yet, Mariella,' he told her grimly. 'When I do return to the villa, we shall discuss it further!'

Mariella didn't risk making any response. There wasn't any need, not unless she wanted to provoke a further quarrel. The frieze was finished; there was nothing now to keep her in Zuran, no reason or need for her to stay, and she had already decided that she was going to make immediate plans to return home!

CHAPTER ELEVEN

'ELLA, you have to go! The prince will be mortally offended if you don't and, besides, just think of the potential commissions you could be losing. I mean, I've done some discreet checking on the guest list for this do, and everyone who is everyone in the horse-racing world will be there, plus some of the classiest A-list celebs on the planet! This is going to be the most prestigious event on the racing calendar this year, and here you are announcing that you don't want to go! I mean, why? You already know just how impressed the prince is with your frieze, and this is going to be its big unveiling. If you'd been hired by the National Gallery itself you couldn't have got yourself more publicity for your work!'

Mariella could hear the exasperation in her agent's voice, and ruefully acknowledged inwardly that she could perfectly understand Kate's feelings.

However, Kate did not know that she had two very good reasons for her reluctance to return to Zuran.

Xavier...and... Instinctively she glanced down her own body. At three months, her pregnancy was not really showing as yet. She and the baby were both perfectly healthy, her doctor had assured her, it was just that being so slight she was not as yet showing very much baby bulge.

'Just wait another couple of months and you'll probably be complaining to me that you feel huge,' she had teased Mariella.

Even now sometimes when she woke up in the morning she had to reassure herself that she was not fantasising, and that she actually was pregnant.

Pregnant… With a baby she already desperately wanted and loved. Her baby! Her baby and Xavier's baby, she reminded herself warily.

But Xavier would never need to know! No one looking at her could possibly know!

And if she was not careful she could potentially be in danger of arousing more suspicions by not returning to Zuran for the extravaganza that was to be the opening of the new enclosure and the first public airing of her frieze than by doing so.

Tanya for one would certainly have something to say to her if she didn't go!

And of course it would be a perfect opportunity for her to see Fleur, whom she still missed achingly. Her niece would also always have a very, very special place in her heart!

But against all this, and weighing very heavily on the other side of the scales, was Xavier. Xavier whom disturbingly she had spent far too much time thinking about since her return home! Mystifyingly and totally contrary to her expectations, not even the official knowledge that she had conceived her much-wanted child had brought an end to the little ache of longing and loneliness that now seemed to haunt both her days and her nights. There was surely no logical reason why she should actually physically ache for Xavier now. And there was certainly no reason why increasingly she should feel such a deep and despairing emotional longing for him. Those kinds of feelings belonged to someone who was in love! And she knew far better than to allow herself to do anything as foolish as fall in love!

She had actually begun to question, in her most emotional and anguished moments, whether what she was feeling could in some way be generated by the baby— a longing on his or her part for the father that he or she was never going to know. She had promised herself that her child would never suffer the anguish of being rejected by his or her father, because she had made sure there would be no father there to reject it. She would make sure right from the start that her baby would know that she would provide all the love it could possibly need! She would bring him or her up to feel so loved, so secure, so wanted, that Xavier's absence would have no impact on their lives whatsoever. Unlike her, her child would never suffer the pain of hearing his or her mother talk with such longing and need about the man who had abandoned them both, as she had had to do. Her child would never feel as she had done that somehow he or she was the cause of that father's absence; that, given the real choice, her mother would have preferred not to have had her and kept the love of the man who had quite simply not wanted the responsibility of a child!

'You must go,' Kate was insisting.

'You must come,' Tanya was pleading.

'Okay, okay, I give in,' she told Kate, grinning as her agent paused in mid-argument to look at her in silence, before breaking into a flurry of relieved plans.

'You'll be staying with us, of course,' Tanya was chattering excitedly as she bustled Mariella outside to the waiting limousine. 'I didn't bring Fleur because she's been cutting another new tooth. It's through now, but we had a bit of a bad night with her. I can't wait for the opening. It's going to be the highlight of our social calendar. Khalid has bought me the most fabulous dress. What are you going to wear? If you haven't got anything yet, we could go shopping—'

'No, it's okay, I've already got an outfit,' Mariella stopped her quickly, mentally grateful for the fact that Kate had insisted on taking her on a whirlwind shopping trip, following her decision to attend the opening, so that she could vet the outfit Mariella would be wearing, to make sure it made enough of the right kind of statement! Her small bulge might not show yet when she was dressed, but someone as close to her as her half-sister had always been would be bound to spot the differences in her body in the intimacy of a changing room with her wearing nothing more than her underwear!

Of course she was going to tell Tanya about her baby—ultimately—once she was safely back in England, and all the questions her sister was bound to ask about just who had fathered her coming baby could be answered over the telephone rather than in person! The last thing Mariella wanted to do was to risk betraying herself by a give-away expression.

She knew exactly what she was going to tell Tanya. She had already decided to claim that her child was the result of artificial insemination, the father an unknown sperm donor.

They were speeding along the highway towards the familiar outskirts of the city.

'How far is it to your new villa, Tanya?' Mariella asked her.

She had been receiving a constant stream of emails from her sister full of excitement about the new villa she and Khalid were having built, and which they had recently been due to move into.

'Oh, it's several miles up the coast from Xavier's. I'm really looking forward to moving into it now, but I must admit I'm a bit worried about how Fleur is going to adapt. She adores Hera, and to her Xavier's villa is her home and so—'

'What do you mean you're looking forward to moving in?' Mariella checked her anxiously. 'I thought you already had!'

'Well, yes, we were supposed to, but then all the furniture hasn't arrived yet, and so we're still living with Xavier. His great-aunt is visiting at the moment as well. You made a real hit with her, Ella—not like me. She's always singing your praises and in fact... I...'

Mariella could feel her heart, not just sinking, but literally plunging to the bottom of her ribcage with an almighty thump before it began to bang against her ribs in frantic panic. She wasn't prepared for this, she admitted. She wasn't armed for it, or protected against it.

The villa was ahead of them. It was too late for her to announce that she had changed her mind, or to demand that she be taken to the centre of the city where she could book into a hotel! The car was sweeping in through the gates.

Hazily Mariella noticed that the red geraniums she remembered tumbling from the urns in the outer courtyard had been changed to a rich vibrant pink to match the colour of the flowers of the ornamental vine softening the walls of the courtyard.

'Leave your luggage for Ali,' Tanya instructed her.

Where was the trepidation she should be feeling? Mariella wondered as, completely contrary to any kind of logic, the moment she stepped into the villa she immediately experienced a sense of well being, a sense of welcome familiarity, as though…as though she had come home?

'We'd better go straight in to see Tante Cecille!' Tanya pulled a face. 'I'll never hear the end of it if we don't. She's even told them in the kitchen to bake some madeleines for you!'

Mariella had to bite down hard on her bottom lip to subdue the threatening weakness of her own emotional response. The last thing she wanted or needed right now was to be reminded in any way of the fact that she was so very much alone, so very bereft of family, unlike Xavier, who was not merely part of a large extended family group, but who also actively shared a large part of his life with them.

Treacherously Mariella found herself thinking about how a child might feel growing up in a household with so many caring adults, with aunts, uncles and cousins to play with…

'Ella, I'm so thrilled that you're here,' Tanya was telling her. 'I've really missed you! You're in the same room you had before. Xavier has given us our own suite of rooms whilst we're living here. Khalid says there's no way that he would agree to us living like they used to with separate men and women's quarters, which is just as well because there's no way I would agree to it either!

'I couldn't do what Xavier does and go into the desert with the tribe.' Tanya gave a small shudder. 'The very thought appalls me. All that sand…and heat! And as for the camels! Ugh!' She pulled a distasteful face. 'Luckily Khalid feels exactly the same way! He can't understand why Xavier lets his life be dominated by a few promises his grandfather made, and neither can I.

If Khalid was head of the family things would be very different...'

'Then perhaps it's as well that he isn't,' Mariella responded protectively, before she could stop herself.

She could see the way Tanya was looking at her, and she felt obliged to explain, 'Xavier is the guardian of some irreplaceable traditions, Tanya, and if he abandoned that responsibility a way of life that could never be resurrected could be totally lost...'

'A way of life? Spending weeks living in the desert, and having to do it every year! No, I can't think of anything worse. It might be traditional, but I still wouldn't do it! Well, there's no way it could ever be my way of life, anyway. I mean, can you imagine any woman wanting to live like that? Could you?'

Mariella didn't even have to pause to think about it.

'Not permanently, no, but in order to preserve something so important, and to support the man I loved, to be with him and share a very, very important part of his life, yes, I could and would.' Mariella hesitated, recognising that there was little point in trying to explain to her sister how much such a return to traditions, to the simplicity of such a lifestyle could do to rejuvenate a person in a very special and intensely personal, almost spiritual sense, to bring them back in touch with certain important realities of life. Tanya simply wouldn't understand.

'Yes?' Tanya stared at her. 'You're mad,' she told her, shaking her head. 'Just like Xavier. In fact...Tante Cecille is quite right. You and Xavier are two of a kind.'

Before Mariella could demand an explanation from Tanya of just how and when their similarities had been discussed, they were in the salon.

'Mariella, how lovely to see you again,' Madame Flavel exclaimed affectionately. Automatically as she embraced her Mariella held in her stomach, just as she had done when she and Tanya had hugged earlier. An automatic reflex, but one that wasn't going to conceal her growing bump for very much longer, Mariella acknowledged ruefully.

Half an hour later, holding Fleur whilst her niece beamed happily up at her, Mariella began to feel a little bit more relaxed. Xavier, after all, would be as keen to avoid spending time with her as she was with him—albeit for very different reasons! She might even not actually see him at all!

Totally involved in making delicious eye contact with Fleur, Mariella was oblivious to what was going on in the rest of the room until she heard Madame Flavel exclaiming happily, 'Ah, there you are, Xavier.'

Xavier! Automatically Mariella spun round, holding tightly onto Fleur more for her own protection than for the baby's, she recognised dizzily as she felt her whole body begin to tremble.

The sensation, the need slicing white-hot through her threw her into shocked panic. She couldn't be feeling like this. *Should* not be feeling like this. Should not be feeling this all-absorbing need to feed hungrily on the sight of every familiar feature, every slight nuance of expression, too greedy for them to savour them with luxurious slowness, aching for them; aching for him so intensely that the pain was sharply physical.

As the girl she had been before, she had fantasised naively about that wanting and about him, imagining, exploring in the privacy of her thoughts the potential of her secret yearnings for Xavier—she had never guessed where those feelings could lead.

But as she was now sharply aware she was not that girl any more. She was now a woman, a woman looking at the man who had been her lover, knowing just how his flesh lay against his bones, how it felt, how it tasted…how he touched and loved. And as that woman she was overwhelmed by the sheer force of her need to go to him, to be with him, to be part of him. Her knowledge of him, instead of slaking her desire, was actually increasing it, tormenting her with intensely intimate memories. She was no longer seeing him as a powerful distant figure, but as a man…*her* man!

But that wasn't possible. What did that mean about her feelings for Xavier?

'Xavier, I was just telling Ella how alike you and she are,' she heard Tanya commenting.

'Alike?'

Mariella could feel his gaze burning into her as he focused on her.

'In your attitudes to things,' Tanya explained. 'Ella, you really ought to have children of your own,' Tanya added ruefully. 'You are a natural mother.'

'I totally agree with you, Tanya.' Madame Flavel nodded.

Mariella could feel her face and then her whole body burning as they all turned to look at her, but it was Xavier's grim scrutiny that affected her the most as his glance skimmed her body, resting on the baby she was holding in her arms. The unbearable poignancy of knowing that in six months' time she would be holding his child as she was holding Fleur right now made her eyes burn with dangerous tears. What on earth was wrong with her? She was behaving as though…

reacting as though…as though she were a woman in love. Totally, hopelessly, helplessly in love. But she wasn't! She wasn't going to let herself be!

Bleakly Xavier watched as Mariella cuddled Fleur. He had told himself that the discovery that she did not return his feelings would be enough to destroy them. And it should have been! But right now, if they had been alone…

The sickening feeling that had accompanied her unwanted thoughts was refusing to go away, and Mariella began to panic. She had suffered some morning sickness in the early weeks of her pregnancy, but these last few weeks she had felt much better. This nausea, though, wasn't anything to do with what was happening inside her body. No, this nausea was caused by her emotions! And what emotions! They surged powerfully inside her, inducing fear and panic, making her want to turn and run.

Automatically she had turned away from Xavier, unable to trust herself to continue facing him. Tanya had run to greet her husband who had just arrived.

'Ella,' Khalid greeted her warmly. 'We are so pleased that you are here, and I warn you that now that you are we shall not allow you to go easily. Tanya is already making plans to persuade you to move permanently to Zuran. Has she told you?'

Move permanently to Zuran! The shock of his disclosure made Mariella sway visibly, her face paling.

Xavier frowned as he saw her reaction. She looked as though she was about to pass out!

'Khalid, get some water,' Xavier demanded sharply, going immediately to Mariella's side and taking Fleur from her.

Just the feel of his hand touching her bare arm made her shudder with longing, and it seemed to Mariella as though the baby in her womb ached with the same longing that she did, for his touch and for his love.

She was vaguely conscious of being steered towards a chair and instructed to sit down, and then of a glass of water being handed to her.

'There's nothing wrong. I'm perfectly all right,' she protested frantically. The last thing she needed right now was to arouse any kind of suspicions about her health!

'Ella, you do look pale,' Tanya was saying worriedly.

'I'm just a bit tired, that's all,' Mariella insisted.

'You will probably feel better once you have had something to eat. We are going to have an informal family dinner this evening.'

'No,' Mariella refused agitatedly. The last thing she felt able to cope with right now was any more time spent in Xavier's company.

'Tanya, I'm sorry, but I just don't feel up to it. I'm rather tired…the flight…'

'Of course, petite, we understand,' Madame Flavel was assuring her soothingly, unintentionally coming to her rescue. 'Don't we, Xavier?' she appealed.

'Perfectly,' Mariella heard Xavier agreeing harshly.

Abruptly Mariella opened her eyes. Her heart was thumping heavily. She had been dreaming about Xavier. She looked at her watch. It was only just gone ten o' clock. The others would probably just be sitting down for their evening meal. Her throat ached and felt raw, tight with the intensity of her emotions.

As she slid her feet out of the bed and padded to the

window to look out into the shadowy garden she shivered in the coolness of the air-conditioning. It was there by the pool that Xavier had massaged her aching shoulders, and she had realised how much she'd wanted him. Because she had wanted his child, not because she loved him.

Her eyes burned dryly with pain. What she was feeling, what she was having to confront now, went way, way beyond the relief of easy tears.

So she was her mother's daughter, after all! She was to suffer the same pain as her mother—a pain she had inflicted on herself! How could she have been so stupid? How could she have been so reckless as to challenge fate? How could she have ignored everything that she knew about herself? Surely somewhere she must have realised that it was impossible for her to give herself to a man with the passionate intensity she had given herself to Xavier and not love him?

All she had wanted was to have a child, she insisted stubbornly. A child? No, what she had wanted was Xavier's child. And that alone should have told her, warned her...

With appalling clarity Mariella suddenly realised what she had done. Not so much to herself but to her child!

One day her child was going to demand to know about its father. When that happened, what answers was she going to be able to give?

Now she could cry. Slow, acid tears of guilt and regret, but it was too late to change things now.

'I'm so sorry,' she whispered, her hands on her stomach. 'Please, please try to forgive me...I love you so much...'

She had stolen the right to choose fatherhood from

Xavier, and she had stolen from her child the right to be fathered…loved.

It was gone midnight when she finally stopped pacing the room and crawled into bed to fall into a shallow, exhausted sleep, riddled with guilt and anguished dreams.

'Well, what do you think? How do I look?' Tanya demanded excitedly as she twirled round in front of Mariella in her new outfit.

'You look fabulous,' Mariella assured her truthfully.

'And so do you,' Tanya told her. Mariella forced a smile.

Her own dress with its simple flowing lines did suit her, but she was far more concerned about how well it concealed her shape than how well she looked in it. In less than half an hour they would be on their way to the gala opening of the prince's new hospitality suite at the racecourse, and Mariella would have given anything not to have to be there!

Tanya, on the other hand, couldn't wait, her excitement more than making up for Mariella's lack of it.

The last three days had been total torture for her. It would have been bad enough simply discovering that she loved Xavier without the additional emotional anguish of having to endure his constant presence. Every time she looked at him the pain grew worse and so did her guilt.

She had hardly been able to eat because of her misery and anxiety, and she couldn't wait to get on the plane that would take her home!

Under different circumstances, although she would have been nervous about the thought of the coming event, it would have been a very different kind of nervousness, caused purely by her anxiety about people's reaction to her work. Right now, she recognised rue-fully, she hardly cared what they thought!

'Come on,' Tanya urged her. 'It's time to go.'

Reluctantly, Mariella got up.

She could feel Xavier's gaze burning into her as she walked into the courtyard where he and Khalid were already standing beside the waiting car.

The hot desert wind tugged at the thin silk layers of her full-length dress and immediately Mariella reached anxiously to hold them away from her body.

To her relief Xavier got into the front of the car, but she was still acutely conscious of him as Ali drove them towards the racecourse. Unlike Xavier, Khalid fa-voured a strong modern male cologne, but she could still smell beneath it the scent of Xavier's skin, and deep down inside her a part of her cried out in an-guished pain and longing, aching despairingly for him.

'Poor Ella, you must be so nervous.' Tanya tried to comfort her, sensing her distress, but to Mariella's re-lief not realising the real cause of it. 'You've hardly eaten a thing since you arrived, and you look so pale.'

'Tanya is right—you do look pale,' Xavier told Mariella grimly several minutes later when they had reached their destination and he had opened the car door for her, leaving her with no alternative but to get out. His hand was beneath her elbow, preventing her from moving away from him. Instinctively Mariella knew that he had been waiting for the opportunity to vent the anger he obviously felt towards her against her. She had seen it in his eyes every time he looked at her, felt it in the tension that crackled between them. 'What's wrong, Mariella? If it isn't food you want, then perhaps it's another appetite you want to have satisfied. Is that it? Are you hungry for sex?' he demanded harshly.

'No,' Mariella denied immediately, trying again to pull away from him. He was making sure that no one else could hear what he was saying to her, she recognised, and making sure too that she could not get away from him.

Had he deliberately waited until now? Chosen this particular time to launch his attack on her, when he knew she couldn't escape from him?

'No?' he taunted her. 'Then why are you trembling so much? Why do you look so hungrily at me when you think I am not aware of you doing so?'

'I am not...I do not,' Mariella replied. She could feel her face starting to burn and her heart beginning to pound.

'You're lying,' Xavier told her softly. 'And don't deny it. Unless you want to provoke me into proving to you that you are! Is that what you want, Mariella?'

'Stop it! Stop doing this to me,' Mariella demanded. She could hear her own voice shaking with emotion and was helplessly aware that it wouldn't be long before her body betrayed her by following suit.

'I spoke to your agent today. She told me that she was sure you'd be thrilled to learn that I want to commission you for a very special project. She certainly was especially when I told her how much I was prepared to pay to secure your exclusive...services.'

Mariella reeled from the shock of his taunting comment.

'Xavier, please,' she begged him fatally, her eyes widening as she saw the look of triumph leaping to life in his eyes.

'Please?' he repeated silkily.

'Xavier, Mariella, come on...' Tanya urged them.

'We're coming. I was just discussing a certain plan with Mariella,' Xavier said smoothly as he guided Mariella toward the throng of people making for the entrance to the suite.

'Well, sister-in-law, I think we can safely say that your frieze is an outstanding success,' Khalid commented, grinning at Mariella. 'Everyone is talking about it and it is very, very impressive!'

Mariella tried to respond enthusiastically, but she felt achingly tired from answering all the questions she had received about the frieze, and, besides, her whole nervous system was still on red alert just in case Xavier should suddenly reappear and continue his cynical verbal torment.

'Khalid and I are going to get something to eat, in a few minutes,' Tanya told her. 'Do you want to come with us?'

Nauseously Mariella shook her head. The last thing she wanted was food. She had been feeling sick all day and her stomach heaved at the very thought.

'Here comes the prince,' Tanya whispered as the royal party appeared.

'Mariella. My congratulations. Everyone is most impressed!'

As she acknowledged his praise Mariella suddenly realised that Xavier was with him. Her feeling of sickness increased, but grimly she refused to submit to it.

'Xavier has just been telling me that he has commissioned you to make a visual record of the everyday life of his people,' the prince was continuing. 'A truly excellent idea!' Smiling at her, he started to move on.

So that was what Xavier had meant! Already dropping her head in deference to the prince, Mariella suddenly raised it, intending to glare at Xavier, but instead she was overcome by a dizzying surge of weakness.

'Ella, what is it? What's wrong?' Tanya demanded anxiously. 'You look as though you're going to faint! Feeling sick…looking like you're going to faint—anyone would think you're pregnant!' Tanya laughed.

As her sister turned away Mariella realised that Xavier was looking straight at her, and she knew immediately from his expression that he had heard Tanya's teasing comment and that somehow he had guessed the truth!

The urge to turn and run was so strong that she suspected if the gallery had not been so crowded she would have done so. But once again Xavier seemed to be able to read her mind because suddenly he was standing beside her.

'Your sister isn't well,' she heard him telling Tanya curtly. 'I'm taking her back to the villa.'

'No,' Mariella protested, but it was too late. Khalid was urging Tanya to go with him to get something to eat, and Xavier was already propelling her towards the exit.

It was impossible for either of them to say anything in the car with Ali driving. 'This way,' Xavier told Mariella grimly once they were back at the villa, stopping her from seeking the sanctuary of her own room as his hand on the small of her back ushered her towards his own suite of rooms.

'You can't do this!' Mariella said shakily. 'I'm a single woman, remember, and—'

'A single woman who is carrying my child!' Xavier

stopped her savagely as he opened the suite door and almost pushed her inside.

Mariella could feel herself starting to tremble. She didn't have the strength for this kind of fight. Not now and probably not ever!

'Xavier, I'm tired. It's been a long day.'

'Why the hell didn't you say something? Or were you hoping that by not eating and by exhausting yourself you could provoke a natural end to it?' he accused, ignoring her plea.

'No,' Mariella denied immediately, horrified. 'No! How dare you say that? I would never...' Tears filled her eyes. 'I wanted this baby,' she told him passionately. 'I...'

Abruptly she stopped, her expression betraying her as she saw the way he was looking at her.

'Would you mind repeating that?' he demanded with dangerous softness.

Nervously Mariella licked her lips.

'Repeat what?' she asked him.

'Don't play games with me Mariella,' he warned her. 'You know perfectly well what I mean. You just said "I wanted this baby"..."wanted," rather than "want," which means...which means that it wasn't just sex you wanted from me, as you claimed, was it?

'What? Nothing to say?' he challenged her bitingly. 'Not even an "it was an accident"?'

Mariella bit down hard on her lower lip.

She wasn't going to demean herself by lying to him!

'You don't have to worry,' she tried to defend herself, her voice wobbling. 'I won't ever make any kind of claims on you, Xavier. I intend to take full responsibility for...for everything. I want to take full responsibility,' she stressed fiercely. 'There's no way I intend to let my baby suffer as I did through having a father who…'

'Your baby?' Xavier stopped her harshly. 'Your baby, Mariella, is my child! My child!'

'No!' Mariella denied immediately. 'This baby has nothing whatsoever to do with you, Xavier. He or she will be completely mine!'

'Nothing to do with me! I don't believe I'm hearing this,' Xavier breathed savagely. 'This baby…my baby has everything to do with me, Mariella. After all, without me he or she just could not exist! I'll make arrangements for us to be married as quickly and as quietly as possible, and then—'

'Married! No!' Mariella refused vehemently, her panic showing in her expression as she confronted him. 'I'm not going to get married, Xavier. Not ever. When my mother married my father, she believed that he loved her, that she could trust him, rely on him…but she couldn't. He left her… He left us both because he didn't want me.'

All the emotions she had been bottling up inside her whooshed out in a despairing stream of agonised denial, even whilst somewhere deep down inside her most guarded private self there was a deep burning pain at the thought of just how very, very much she wanted Xavier's total commitment for her baby and for herself. His total commitment and his enduring love! The pain of her own self-knowledge was virtually unbearable. She ached for him to simply take her in his arms and hold her safe, to keep her safe for ever, and yet at the same time her own self-conditioning was urging her to deny and deride those feelings to protect herself.

'I am not your father, Mariella, and where my child is concerned—' his mouth tightened '—in Zuran it is a father whose rights are paramount. I would be within my legal rights in ensuring that you are not permitted to leave the country with my child—either before or after his or her birth!'

Distraught, Mariella demanded passionately, 'Why are you doing this? Your own aunt told me that you had sworn never to marry or have children; that you didn't want a wife or children.'

'No,' Xavier stopped her curtly. 'It is true that I had decided not to marry, but not because I didn't want... The reason I had chosen not to marry was because I believed I could never find a woman who would love me as a man, with fire and passion and commitment, and that I wouldn't be able to find a woman also who would understand and accept my responsibilities to my people. I didn't think that such a woman could exist!'

'And because she doesn't...because I am carrying your child, you're prepared to marry me instead, is that it? I can't do it, Xavier. I won't, I won't be married, just because of the baby.' Her voice began to wobble betrayingly as her emotions overwhelmed her and to her own humiliation tears flooded her eyes and began to roll down her face. Helplessly Mariella lifted her hands to her face to shield herself, unable to bear Xavier's contemptuous response to her distress. It must be baby hormones that were making her cry like this, making her feel so weak and vulnerable!

'Mariella.'

Mariella froze with shock as she felt the warmth of Xavier's exhaled breath against her skin, as he crossed the space between them and took her in his arms.

'Don't!' His voice was rough with pain. 'I can't bear the thought of knowing that you and my child, the two people I love the most, will be lost to me, but I can't bear either knowing that I have forced you to stay with me against your will. When you came to me in the desert, gave yourself to me...it was as though you had read my mind. Shared my thoughts and my feelings, known how much I had wanted us to be together, and known too that I had been waiting for the right opportunity to approach you and tell you how I felt, but I was conscious of what had happened during your own childhood with your father. I wanted to win your belief in me, your trust of me...before I revealed to you how much I wanted to ask you to share my life! I knew how strong your sense of commitment was, your sense of responsibility, and I knew that the future of my people would rest safely in your hands. I thought that together you and I could...but I was wrong, as you made very clear to me... You didn't love me; you didn't even really want me. You merely wanted someone to father your child.

'I want and need both of you here with me more than I can find the words to tell you, but I cannot bear to see you so distressed. I shall make arrangements for you to return to England if that is what you want, but what I would ask you is that you allow me to play at least some part in my child's life, however small. I shall, of course, make financial provision for both of you...that is not just my duty, but my right! But at least once a year I should like your permission to see my child. To spend time with him or her. If necessary I shall come to your country to do so. And...'

Mariella fought to take in what he was saying. Xavier wanted her. Xavier loved her. In fact he loved her so much that he was prepared to put her needs and wishes above his own!

A new feeling began to whisper softly through her,

a soft warmth that permeated every cell of her body, melting away all the tiny frozen particles of mistrust and pain that had been with her from the very first moment she had known about her father. A feeling so unfamiliar, so heady and euphoric that it made her literally tremble with happiness, and excitement unfurled and grew inside.

Instinctively her hand touched her belly. Could her baby feel what she was feeling? Was he or she right now uncurling and basking in the same glow of happiness that was engulfing her?

Xavier's hand covered hers and that small gesture brought immediate emotional tears to her eyes as she turned to look at him without any attempt to hide her emotions from him.

'I didn't know you loved me,' she whispered.

'You know now,' Xavier responded.

She could see the bleakness in his eyes and the pain. Her body could feel the warmth of his hand even through her own. Gently she pulled her own hand away and leaned into him so that he could feel the growing swell of their child, her gaze monitoring his immediate and intense reaction.

Xavier would never do what her father had done, instinctively she knew that, just as she knew too how much time she had wasted, how much that was so infinitely precious to her she had risked and nearly lost because of her frightened refusal to allow herself to believe that not all men were like her father.

Alongside her bubbling happiness she could feel another emotion she had to struggle to identify. It was freedom, she recognised; freedom from the burden she had been carrying around with her for so long, and it was Xavier who had given her that freedom by giving her his love, by being man enough, strong enough to reveal his vulnerability to her!

She took a deep breath and then held tightly to her courage and even more tightly to Xavier's arm.

'It isn't true what I said,' she told him simply. 'It wasn't just sex. I tried to pretend it was to myself because I was too afraid to admit how I really felt, but I think I knew even before, and then afterwards when I still wanted you...' Her skin turned a warm rose as she saw the way he was looking at her.

'Don't look at me like that,' she protested. 'Not yet, not until I've finished telling you... Otherwise...'

'Still wanted, in the past tense or...' Xavier pressed her huskily.

'Still wanted then,' Mariella informed him primly. 'And still want now,' she added, her own voice suddenly as husky and liquid with emotion as his had been. 'I still want you, Xavier!' she repeated. 'And I don't just want you, I need you as well. Need you and love you,' she finally managed to say, her voice so low that he had to bend his head to catch her shaky admission.

'You love me? But do you trust me, Mariella? Do you believe me when I tell you that I shall never, ever let you down or give you cause to doubt me? Do you believe me when I tell you that you and our child...our children, will always have my love and my commitment?'

Mariella closed her eyes and then opened them again.

'Yes,' she replied firmly, and her melting look of love told him that she meant it!

'Xavier,' she protested unconvincingly as he started to kiss her. 'The others will be coming back.'

'Shall I stop, then?' he asked her, brushing his lips tormentingly against her own.

'Mmm… No…' Mariella responded helplessly, sighing in soft pleasure as his hand covered her breast, his thumb probing the aroused sensitivity of her nipple. Her whole body turned liquid with desire, making her cling eagerly to him.

'Every night I've thought about you like this,' Xavier told her rawly. 'Wanted you…ached for you in my arms. Every night, and every day, and if I'd known that there was the smallest chance that you felt the same I would never have let you go. I warn you, Ella, that now that I do know I will never let you go.'

'I will never want you to,' Mariella responded emotionally. 'Take me to bed, Xavier,' she begged him urgently. 'Take me to bed and show me that this isn't all just a dream…'

She was in his arms and being carried from the salon into his bedroom almost before the words had left her mouth. And even if she had wanted to retract them it would have been impossible for her to do so with Xavier kissing her the way that he was, with all the passion and love, all the commitment she now recognised that she had secretly ached for all along.

EPILOGUE

'WELL, what do you think of your anniversary present?' Mariella asked Xavier lightly, whilst she watched him with a secret anxiety she was trying hard to hide.

She had been working on this special gift for him on and off ever since their marriage, only breaking off for their six-month-old son's birth and the early weeks of his life.

Xavier shook his head, as though he found it hard to comprehend what he was seeing. 'I knew you were working on something, but this...'

The stern note in his voice broke through her self-control, forcing her to reveal how much his approval meant to her. 'You don't like it—?'

'Like it! Mariella.' Reaching for her, Xavier wrapped her tightly in his arms.

'There is nothing, excluding your sweet self and our noisy and demanding young son, that I would value more,' he told her emotionally as he swung her round in his arms so that they could both look at the series of drawings she had spent the early hours of the morning displaying around their private salon to surprise him when he woke up on this, their anniversary morning.

As a wedding present from her new husband Mariella had asked to be allowed to travel in the desert with the tribe. Conscious of her pregnancy, Xavier had initially been reluctant to agree, but Mariella had been insistent. It had been on that journey that she had made the secret preliminary sketches for what was now a visual documentation of the tribe's way of life, a visual documentation that betrayed, not only her fine eye for detail, but also her love for the man whose people she had drawn.

'I do have a gift for you, although I haven't followed Tanya's advice and booked a luxury holiday,' Xavier told her ruefully.

Following the direction of his amused glance, Mariella laughed.

Fleur, who was now walking was sitting on the floor next to her six-month-old cousin, the pair of them deep in some personal exchange, which involved lots of shared giggles and some noisy hand-clapping from Ben.

'Don't you dare do any such thing. There's no way I want to be parted from these two!'

With Tanya and Khalid living around the corner, both the families saw a lot of each other, and the two young cousins could grow up together.

'I may have another present for you,' Mariella announced semi-hesitantly, the way her glance lingered on their son informing Xavier of just what she meant.

'What? We said we'd wait.'

'I know…but this time it's your fault and not mine. Remember your birthday, when you didn't want to wait until…'

'Mmm.' He did a rapid mental calculation. 'So in another seven months, then…'

'I think so… Do you mind?'

'Mind? Me? No way. Do you?'

'I've got my fingers crossed that I'm right,' Mariella admitted. 'Although I'm pretty sure that I am, and if I'm not…' she gave him a flirtatious look '…then I'm sure we can find a way of ensuring that I soon am! Anyway, what about *my* anniversary present? You still haven't told me what it is.'

'Come with me,' Xavier instructed her, bending to pick up their son and hand him to Mariella before lifting Fleur up into his own arms.

'Close your eyes and hold onto me,' Xavier said as he led her out into their own private courtyard, and through it to the new courtyard that had been developed behind it.

Mariella could smell the roses before he allowed her to open her eyes, and once he did so she drew in her breath in delight as she saw the new garden he had been having designed for her as a special surprise.

A softer and far more modern planting plan had been adopted for the new garden than the one favoured by Xavier's grandmother. The design was reminiscent of an English country garden with the flower beds filled with a variety of traditional plants, but it was the wonderful scent of the roses that most caught her attention.

'They're called "Eternity",' Xavier told her softly as she bent her head to touch the velvet-soft petals of the rose closest to her. 'And I promise that I shall love you for eternity, Mariella, and beyond it. My love for you is…eternal!'

Warm tears bathed Mariella's eyes as she smiled at him.

'And mine for you!' she whispered lovingly to him.

Silently, they walked through the garden together, his arm around her drawing her close, her head resting against his shoulder, the children in their arms.

The world's bestselling romance series.

HARLEQUIN®
Presents

Seduction and Passion Guaranteed!

Coming soon...
To the rescue...armed with a ring!

Modern-Day Knights

Marriage is their mission!
Look out for more stories of
Modern-Day Knights...

Coming next month:
NATHAN'S CHILD
by Anne McAllister
#2333
Coming in August
**AT THE SPANIARD'S
PLEASURE**
by Jacqueline Baird
#2337

**Pick up a Harlequin
Presents® novel and
you will enter a world
of spine-tingling
passion and provocative,
tantalizing romance!**

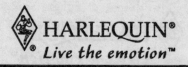

Available wherever Harlequin books are sold.

HARLEQUIN®
Live the emotion™

Visit us at www.eHarlequin.com

HPMDNNC

New York Times bestselling author

PENNY JORDAN

and

SANDRA MARTON

Bring you two tales of glamour, sophistication and international romance in...

For Love or Money

Featuring a classic Penny Jordan story, along with a brand-new novel by favorite author Sandra Marton.

Look for it in July 2003 wherever paperbacks are sold.

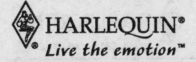

HARLEQUIN®
Live the emotion™

Visit us at www.eHarlequin.com

PHFLOM

The world's bestselling romance series.

Seduction and Passion Guaranteed!

Every book is part of a miniseries in 2003.
These are just some of the exciting themes you can expect...

Your dream ticket to the vacation of a lifetime!

Tall, dark—and ready to marry!

They're guaranteed to raise your pulse!

They're the men who have everything—except a bride....

Marriage is their mission....

Legally wed, but he's never said, "I love you..."

They speak the language of passion

Passion™

Sophisticated spicy stories— seduction and passion guaranteed

Pick up a Harlequin Presents® novel and you will enter a world of spine-tingling passion and provocative, tantalizing romance!

Available wherever Harlequin books are sold.

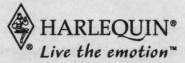

Live the emotion™

Visit us at www.eHarlequin.com

HPMINP03

eHARLEQUIN.com

Sit back, relax and enhance your romance with our great magazine reading!

- **Sex and Romance!** Like your romance *hot?* Then you'll *love* the sensual reading in this area.

- **Quizzes!** Curious about your lovestyle? His commitment to you? Get the answers here!

- **Romantic Guides and Features!** Unravel the mysteries of love with informative articles and advice!

- **Fun Games!** Play to your heart's content....

Plus...romantic recipes, top ten lists, Lovescopes...and more!

Enjoy our online magazine today— visit www.eHarlequin.com!

INTMAG

If you enjoyed what you just read,
then we've got an offer you can't resist!

Take 2 bestselling
love stories FREE!
Plus get a FREE surprise gift!

Clip this page and mail it to Harlequin Reader Service®

IN U.S.A.	IN CANADA
3010 Walden Ave.	P.O. Box 609
P.O. Box 1867	Fort Erie, Ontario
Buffalo, N.Y. 14240-1867	L2A 5X3

YES! Please send me 2 free Harlequin Presents® novels and my free surprise gift. After receiving them, if I don't wish to receive anymore, I can return the shipping statement marked cancel. If I don't cancel, I will receive 6 brand-new novels every month, before they're available in stores! In the U.S.A., bill me at the bargain price of $3.57 plus 25¢ shipping & handling per book and applicable sales tax, if any*. In Canada, bill me at the bargain price of $4.24 plus 25¢ shipping & handling per book and applicable taxes**. That's the complete price and a savings of at least 10% off the cover prices—what a great deal! I understand that accepting the 2 free books and gift places me under no obligation ever to buy any books. I can always return a shipment and cancel at any time. Even if I never buy another book from Harlequin, the 2 free books and gift are mine to keep forever.

106 HDN DNTZ
306 HDN DNT2

Name	(PLEASE PRINT)	
Address	Apt.#	
City	State/Prov.	Zip/Postal Code

* Terms and prices subject to change without notice. Sales tax applicable in N.Y.
** Canadian residents will be charged applicable provincial taxes and GST.
  All orders subject to approval. Offer limited to one per household and not valid to
  current Harlequin Presents® subscribers.
  ® are registered trademarks of Harlequin Enterprises Limited.

PRES02   ©2001 Harlequin Enterprises Limited

"Georgette Heyer has given me great pleasure over the years
in my reading, and rereading, of her stories."
—#1 *New York Times* bestselling author Nora Roberts

Experience the wit, charm
and irresistible characters of

GEORGETTE
HEYER

creator of the modern Regency romance genre

Enjoy six new collector's editions with forewords
by some of today's bestselling romance authors:

**Catherine Coulter, Kay Hooper, Stella Cameron,
Diana Palmer, Stephanie Laurens and Linda Howard.**

The Grand Sophy
March

The Foundling
April

Arabella
May

The Black Moth
June

These Old Shades
July

Devil's Cub
August

Available at your favorite retail outlet.

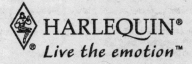

HARLEQUIN®
Live the emotion™

Visit us at www.eHarlequin.com

PHGH

COOPER'S CORNER

The intimacy of
Cooper's Corner...
The high stakes of
Wall Street...

Trade
Secrets

Containing two
full-length novels
based on the bestselling
Cooper's Corner continuity!

Jill Shalvis
C.J. Carmichael

Many years ago, a group of
MBA students at Harvard made
a pact—each to become a CEO
of a Fortune 500 company
before reaching age forty.
Now their friendships,
their loves and even their
lives are at stake....

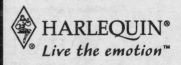

HARLEQUIN®
Live the emotion™

Visit us at www.eHarlequin.com

PHTS

The world's bestselling romance series.

HARLEQUIN®
Presents

Seduction and Passion Guaranteed!

Your dream ticket to the vacation of a lifetime!

Why not relax and allow Harlequin Presents® to whisk you away
to stunning international locations with our new miniseries...

**Where irresistible men and sophisticated women
surrender to seduction under the golden sun.**

Don't miss this opportunity to
experience glamorous lifestyles
and exotic settings in:

**Robyn Donald's
THE TEMPTRESS OF TARIKA BAY
on sale July, #2336**

**THE FRENCH COUNT'S MISTRESS
by Susan Stephens
on sale August, #2342**

**THE SPANIARD'S WOMAN
by Diana Hamilton
on sale September, #2346**

**THE ITALIAN MARRIAGE
by Kathryn Ross
on sale October, #2353**

FOREIGN AFFAIRS... A world full of passion!

**Pick up a Harlequin Presents® novel and you will enter a world
of spine-tingling passion and provocative, tantalizing romance!**

Available wherever Harlequin books are sold.

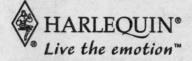

HARLEQUIN®
Live the emotion™

Visit us at www.eHarlequin.com

HPFAMA